THE WIFE HE NEEDED

A Clearwater Romance - Book Three

MEGAN MCCOY

Published by Blushing Books
An Imprint of
ABCD Graphics and Design, Inc.
A Virginia Corporation
977 Seminole Trail #233
Charlottesville, VA 22901

Megan McCoy
The Wife He Needed

EBook ISBN: 978-1-64563-551-2
Print ISBN: 978-1-64563-545-1
v1

Chapter 1

Jordyn Green looked around her – her! – shop. Or what would be her shop soon. Right now, it was just four empty rooms and a dream. She didn't even have a name yet, which was strange considering how long she'd been dreaming, wishing and planning all of this. Not one name just felt right yet. It was coming down to a time crunch though. She needed to get the sign for out front, her business cards, publicity for social media, and all kinds of things ordered soon. She didn't want anything cutesy, like The Sweet Shop, she wasn't a cutesy kind of person. Naming her bakery after her Grandma Rose was an option, but Rose didn't really imply bakery. Today was Monday and she had given herself till Friday to find the name. After all, opening day was November first and that was only three months away!

She set up her temporary office, a folding table and three chairs, and put her laptop on it. She was in business! Well, not yet. Her friend, Lucy, was coming by in a few minutes to see her new place. She'd signed the paperwork while Lucy was off on her honeymoon; she'd gotten back yesterday and wanted to run by this morning while she was out doing errands. Jordyn couldn't wait to show her around.

Looking out the huge front window onto Clearwater's little town square, she smiled, imagining watching the seasons change from that window for the next however many years. The outside of the square had, at one time, been the heart of the town, with everything from a grocery store, to chain stores, small mom and pop shops, coffee shops where people gathered before work in the mornings, the library, and the requisite barber shop where men whiled away many afternoons. Like many towns, it had withered away as the big box stores and the mall came to town, but in the last few years, it had started rebuilding. The town council had been putting in a lot of effort to make sure it did and she felt very pleased to be part of bringing back the heart to the city. The small park across the street held many concerts in the summer, plus charity events, food trucks and, of course, that was where the kids all greeted Santa every season. Right now, the fountain sparkled, the trees were green and the grass lush. When she opened, the leaves would be wearing their brilliant fall colors and perhaps falling. People would be gearing up for winter and the holiday season.

Jordyn envisioned her little shop as a morning meeting place for coffee and donuts or a muffin before work. Where busy moms picked up their child's birthday cake. The place where young brides – or older brides, for that matter – came to pick out their wedding cake. The small room off to the side of this bigger one would be wonderful for cake tastings, small bridal showers, and maybe, eventually, luncheons or teas.

Looking up, she saw Lucy parking right in front of her – her! – shop and almost danced inside. That was Lucy for you and it looked like being married agreed with her. She seemed to be almost glowing.

Walking to the door, Jordyn opened it. "Lucy! Come on in! How was the honeymoon?"

She fingered the elastic band in her pocket. She really should braid her hair before she got busy this morning. It felt so good to have it down for once though. Tight braids were good for work, but sometimes her scalp just needed a break.

"It was fantastic! I'm so glad to be home though; I'm on my way to pick up Gypsy and Juliet from Joni's house." Those were her two little dogs, who were the most spoiled creatures Jordyn had ever met. "But I needed to see you to say congratulations, and see what you have here!" Lucy hugged her, unexpectedly, and said, "I'm so very happy for you!"

"Thank you so much," Jordyn said. "I really didn't think I'd be doing this for about five more years. I've been saving, but when Grandma Rose left me that bit of inheritance, well, I decided that was it. It was time. This place sort of fell into my lap and so far everything is coming together like it was meant to be."

Lucy laughed. "Well, I saw what Ellie and Mike went through when they built their house, but I hope this goes smoothly for you. At least you have walls! So what are the plans?"

"Well!" Jordyn began, "This room, of course, will be the show room. I'm thinking a display case along that wall and a counter here where people pick up things, a coffee and tea station here, then a few small tables and maybe a longer table for the morning coffee drinkers to gather before work."

"Maybe a big table in front of the window to put the baked item of the day for people to see out the window?" Lucy interrupted. "Or a fancy wedding cake to show off?"

"Maybe," Jordyn said. "I am eager to see what the designer says."

"The designer." Lucy stopped and grabbed her arm. "The. Designer?"

Jordyn smiled a little and shrugged. "Well, she's good."

"Oh, I know she's good, she's really good. But, Jordyn!"

"I know," Jordyn said. "It will be fine."

"It's Miranda!" Lucy said. "How will that be fine? She's going to squish you like a bug."

"She's not that bad," Jordyn protested, trying not to feel uneasy. "Anyway, this will be the kitchen. I need her because I don't know all the rules and codes and things like she does."

"I never said she didn't know what she was doing," Lucy said. "How about this room?" They walked into the back of the store.

"Half office, half walk-in freezer and half pantry," Jordyn said.

"I'm not a math major, well, technically I was a finance major, but I really don't think that works out," Lucy said.

"That is totally not my problem. The designer has to figure out how to get three halves out of a room," Jordyn said as they walked back to the front of the store. "And this little room, I can see for cake tastings and small bridal lunches and things. There's the bathroom over there. It needs remodeling badly."

Lucy opened and closed the door. "That's an understatement." Going back into the front room, she glanced out the window.

"Look, Jordyn! It's Paul Bunyan in the flesh and on our square!"

Jordyn walked over and looked out the window. "It is," she agreed. A man walked – no, strode – down the street on the park side of the square. He looked huge. Tall, bearded, massive, jeans and boots, a work shirt rolled up to his elbows and all he needed was an axe over his shoulder and maybe a big blue ox to complete the picture. "He's one gorgeous specimen of lumberjack, isn't he?"

"Well, he's no Max," the newlywed said. "Jordyn, he's coming here!"

"He's just crossing the street," Jordyn said, her heart unexpectedly hammering. Wasn't he?

"If he was just crossing the street, he would have gone to the corner where there are crosswalks made for that purpose, instead of crossing in the middle of the road. Nope, he's coming here," Lucy insisted. "Don't worry, I'll save you!"

"From what?" Jordyn asked. He was coming here! Walking right up to her door. "Do you think he's here to ravish me or something?"

"Ravish?" Lucy giggled. "Hello, sir, can we help you?" she asked as he knocked once and walked in the door. In person he was even more imposing than when striding down the street. Jordyn tried not to stare. At six three, she had thought Ellie's husband Mike was tall. This one had a few more inches on him and a lot more muscle. He was a mountain man! There was a tattoo snaking down one of his arms, and for some reason, she really wanted to see the rest of it. Did he have any more? Where?

"Hello, I'm Ben and am supposed to meet Miranda here," he said.

"I'm Miranda," Jordyn blurted out, then blushed and said, "I mean, Miranda is supposed to meet me. Meet here. Come here. Miranda is going to be here. I'm Jordyn." She wished she was Miranda though, for some reason. Or could fall through the floor. Her cheeks felt so hot. What was wrong with her?

Ben looked at her almost quizzically, then smiled and he suddenly didn't look as intimidating anymore.

"Miranda is always late," he said conversationally, as if she just hadn't stuck both feet in her mouth. "It isn't one of her best qualities."

"She's a very good designer, though," Jordyn said. She was defending Miranda, exactly why?

"That she is," he agreed and folded his arms. She tried not to gawk at the muscles. Lucky Miranda! She really couldn't see the fashionable designer who always wore what they called 'power suits' and whose hair and nails were done to perfection with this man who wore jeans and boots and had a tattoo and a beard and, well, opposites attract. This opposite though? She needed to stop staring at those arms.

Lucy said, "Well, it was really nice to meet you, Ben. I hope you and Miranda hook up soon." She turned and grinned at Jordyn and said, "I really have to go get my girls. Good luck this morning; call me later!"

"Oh, you know I will," Jordyn said.

She watched Lucy leave and turned to Ben as he looked around a little bit. "So what are you doing in here?" he asked.

"Waving my magic wand, throwing my magic checkbook at it and turning it into a bakery. Thus Miranda," she said, itching to ask him about him. Why not? What could it hurt? "So how do you know Miranda?" she asked.

"She hired me to do contract work for her. I just recently moved to town and we'd worked together before."

"So you will be working here?" Oh be still her heart!

"If we're hired," he said easily and smiled at her again, making her knees tremble. Just look at him! She had to get herself under control. He had implied he was 'with' Miranda and she had no intention of getting on Miranda's bad side. She'd heard too many rumors.

"I have an in with the boss," she told him. "You probably have it in the bag. You know, if Miranda ever shows up."

"Oh, she always shows up," he said. "Always late and never mentioning it unless you do. Then she blows it off like it was nothing. Randy's time is more important than anyone else's." He seemed to know her well.

"Well, as long as we all realize that," she said, then laughed. "Here comes the woman of the hour now." They both watched Miranda walk across the street, but down at the corner to cross at the crosswalk, unlike Ben, in her red high heels and pale pink power suit. She had to work out on one of those calf machines at the gym. The woman had gorgeous legs. Why had she noted that? Because she was staring at her walking so she wouldn't stare at Ben like a fool? Maybe.

Miranda walked in the door without knocking and looked around, not quite smiling, not quite smirking. Jordyn suddenly felt anxious, as if she'd failed somehow.

"Randy, you are late, as usual," Ben said.

"Ben, you are dressed like a bum, as always," Miranda retorted. "Hello, Jordyn, I can't wait to see what you have here!"

"Hello, Miranda. I'm looking forward to seeing what you can do for me." Hmmm. That sounded very formal.

"I see you've met my general contractor, and brother from another mother, Ben," she said. "He's a little rough around the edges but he's very good at what he does. I decided with business booming the way it is, it would be an asset to my clients to create my own contracting crew. Ben is the best I know, despite how he dresses."

"Oh, shucks, Randy," Ben shuffled his feet like he was embarrassed but winked at Jordyn, which made her smile. "The pretty things you say."

Not that it mattered one iota, but Jordyn couldn't tell if they were a thing or not. She listened to them banter as they walked around the building and she told them of her dream. "And I need it all done before November first, because that is opening day," she said. "What do you think? Can it happen? Maybe the week before so I can do a soft opening?"

Miranda stopped typing on her tablet. "When?"

"November first," she said.

"Jordyn, seriously? That's three months away. A job like this would usually take five to eight!"

"Really? I really want, no, need, to be open downtown for the holiday season," she said, feeling utterly stricken. She'd thought three months was a long lead time. It seemed like forever to her. Ages before she could open her doors. She hadn't even given notice at her day jobs yet!

"I can aim for, maybe December first," Miranda said. "What do you think, Ben?"

"Well, let's work out figures and plans, and then make an estimate," he said. "Jordyn, we will do the best we can, though."

"How soon can I have the figures and plans?" Jordyn asked, her head spinning.

"Day after tomorrow," Miranda said confidently. "Same time, same place?"

Jordyn nodded. Okay. She'd see what they had to say, and as soon as possible she'd give notice to her clients where she worked as a private chef. After that, she'd find out how to renovate an old brick building into a sweet modern bakery on YouTube because everyone knew that was where you could learn anything. She'd throw sweat equity into this place and if she had to work day and night, well, then she would. Plus she had friends. Her friends would pitch in now and then when they could, she felt certain. Especially if she fed them. If she was going to do this dream, she was going to go all in. Plus, working side by side with Ben did not sound bad at all.

Though, she reminded herself, Miranda. She was not a homewrecker, and they obviously had something. The last thing she wanted or needed now was drama. What did brother from another mean? Were they step-siblings? Half? Best friends with romance and that was just a saying? What did it matter? It didn't. She had a new business to open. Sure, she could fantasize about the hot contractor, not a darn thing wrong with that, but no more. Nothing else. It could be fun, she decided. Fantasy men were as much fun as real ones anyway.

You never had to pick up fantasy men's socks or get up and make them a sandwich or explain why you spent too much on a pair of shoes. Fantasy men just approved of every little thing you did. Well, unless they didn't and put their big, strong, dominant foot down and made you shiver delightedly. However, once again, there was a fantasy man and then the real man. Real men weren't like that. Real men just complained. They didn't know about strong and dominant.

Real men got pissed off at you and made you feel horrible. They put you down and they made you scared. She'd seen it before, and she had no desire for that. She would just enjoy her fantasy man, and the eye candy that was Ben, the mountain man. It was a good thing he was with Miranda. A very good thing. Yes. She would convince herself of that before she saw him again. They spent the next hour going over and over the four little rooms with Miranda and Ben both making copious notes. What could they be writing down?

"What is that door to?" Miranda had asked in the back hallway.

"It goes upstairs. I'm not doing anything with it right now." Miranda nodded and scribbled more down. It was a door! Why did it take what seemed like three pages of notes?

"All right, Jordyn. I'll be back day after tomorrow, and will have the plans and figures and a timeline then and we can make some final decisions." She pulled paperwork out of her satchel and handed it to her. "Here is my contract. You can read it over and we will discuss it at our next meeting. Bring your checkbook. Or, well, I take cards, too."

Why did she feel like Miranda was the one in charge and was hiring her, instead of the other way around? Miranda just was that way. She had yet to meet the person who thought she was equal to Miranda. Everyone felt a little less than when they came away from a meeting with her. But everyone raved about what a fantastic job she did. Her business was apparently booming, despite her personality. Really, there was nothing you could put your finger on that made her disagreeable, but just, well, as Ellie had said, it was just the way she was.

"I'll see you for dinner," Ben said to Miranda. "I want to go take another look at those pipes in that bathroom before I do any estimates."

Miranda didn't even bother to answer him but gave him a wave and walked out the door.

"She's something else, isn't she?" Ben said, watching her walk away.

"She's a little intimidating," Jordyn said. "I mean, she is very nice."

Ben laughed. "I've known her all my life. I know what you mean. There isn't anything you can say 'ow, that was mean' or 'what was that about?' but still, you know she thinks she's better than you."

Jordyn laughed, but felt unsure how to respond to that. He was with Miranda, somehow. Dating? Married? They were having dinner together anyway.

"Come on. Show me which pipes you need to look at," she said as they walked back toward the bathroom.

"Do you really think it will take five months?" she asked him. "I had no clue it would take that long." She thought she was prepared for this bakery. Apparently not. She didn't even have a name! Or a realistic timeline on renovations. On TV they got it done in what seemed like a few days.

"Don't know yet," he said, opening the door to the stinky room, as she called it.

"I'll need to see the copy of the inspection report Miranda has, and do a little poking around, and then see what she has in mind to do, before I can give you a real time estimate. Luckily, it doesn't seem you need any walls taken down. That isn't as easy as it looks on TV."

"Is it as fun as it looks on TV?" she asked him.

"Oh, yeah. Even more," he said, and moved into the bathroom. A few minutes later he came out and said, "Good news."

Jordyn almost sagged with relief. Then covered her mouth not to laugh. She wasn't expecting bad news, was she? No. Then why did 'good news' make her feel like a weight got lifted off? Because she already stressed over the time frame? Probably.

"What is it?"

"Your pipes are in good condition. Not going to have to be replaced. If the rest of the place is in as good shape, you got yourself a good deal."

Jordyn almost beamed. Why did his approval mean so much to her? It didn't. It was only that he knew construction and she'd made a good buy.

"I just hope you can make it into something decent," she said. "Right now, it is a pretty sad little bathroom."

"That it is," he agreed. "That's up to Miranda though. I just do what the boss tells me to do."

Yeah. Miranda.

"Do you have a partner or anything?" he asked her.

What kind of question was that? Or did he need to know if he had still another person to answer to? That was probably all it was. "Nope. This is a one woman show. Well, I have a couple of people who will work for me part time, but I'm the one and only owner. I make all the final decisions."

He laughed and she felt utterly charmed by his low guffaw. "And then you hired Miranda and now you know better."

Jordyn smiled, a little ruefully. "I guess that's true. The

upside of that is I know I will have a great space when she's done."

He nodded in agreement as he typed something more into his tablet. "Owning your own business at your age. You're doing good for a youngster," he said.

Giggling escaped her. She hadn't been carded in years. No one thought she was young. "You are so sweet, but I'm far from a youngster. I turned twenty-eight last week, in fact. See, almost over the hill!"

He looked at her and gave another low chuckle. "Well, now that you mention it, I can see how ancient you are. I'm sorry, ma'am. Didn't mean any disrespect."

"You are forgiven," she said as grandly as she could manage. Not that it was any of his business but, "I've been saving for years for this and when my grandma passed a few months ago, she left me a little to invest in my business."

"I'm sorry about your grandma," he said, which surprised her. She'd thought he was simply worried about being paid.

"Thank you. She'd suffered the last few years, so it was time. But it is still hard, you know, even when you expect it."

He put his tablet down and looked into her eyes. "I do know. Slow or fast, it is always hard when it's final."

Jordyn nodded, blinking back unexpected tears. "I'd like to incorporate her name into the building name or logo or something," she said. "But I haven't found the right way to do it yet."

"You don't have a name or a logo yet?" he asked, sitting down in one of the folding chairs.

Shaking her head, she said, "I gave myself till Friday to come up with the right name and a logo."

"You know outside signs can be a couple of months lead time, depending on where you get them made, right?"

"Why did I think three months was a really long lead time?" she moaned. "I honestly thought I'd be rattling around in here in September or early October bored out of my mind, wishing I was open already."

Ben laughed. "Well, we do what we can, but yeah. You need to make that decision and get that sign ordered this week so I can get it up for you and you can start creating a little buzz. I know a couple of places that do a good job with that, so depending on what you come up with, I can order it for you if you want."

She nodded. Why had she thought there was a mythical sign place, sort of like Amazon that just had signs ready to ship on a second's notice? Of course it would have to be personally made, just for her and her shop.

"I'll have a decision for you when we meet the day after tomorrow," she said.

"Good girl," he said. "And I'm sure Miranda will have a whole bunch more things for you to decide."

Why did his good girl in that tone he said it in make her want to wiggle? Shouldn't she be offended? It was those muscles, she decided and that fascinating tattoo. That was all. He was pure eye candy in the best of ways. She'd have a fun, few months just fantasizing, which, as she reminded herself, was more fun than being with a real man anyway. It would be not only delightful but very safe for her heart. "I better get moving," he said. "The boss lady keeps me on a short leash."

Jordyn smiled. "I imagine she does." That did not feel, well, like anything. It was a non-issue to her. "Good to meet you, Ben," she said. "Looking forward to working with you."

"Same here, Miss Jordyn," he said. "This town looks like a great place to start a new life."

"It is," she told him as they both stood up. "You'll see. Welcome to Clearwater."

"Thanks," he said. "I'll see you in a couple of days."

"You will," she said and watched him walk out the door and across the street. Lucy wouldn't be happy he didn't use the crosswalk, but Lucy was such a rule follower. Personally, she didn't mind watching him stride across the street.

Shaking her head, she started gathering her things and then walked around turning out lights. "I'll be back," she promised her empty shop. "With brand new plans and a brand new name for you. We are going to make memories here, me and you." And she didn't feel a bit silly talking to walls, she thought, as she locked her front door behind her and headed off to her job. They were her walls, after all.

―――――

"Rose's Cakes of Clearwater. What do you think? Is it too long?" Jordyn spoke into the phone to her friend Ellie as she drove home later that day. Ellie was the city manager and she knew things about things.

"Maybe just Cakes of Clearwater and use a rose as a logo to honor your grandma?"

"Yeah, I like that," Jordyn said. "Why is this so hard?"

"Beats me, the only business I ever named was my realty business and that was pretty easy. "Thompson's Realty. Easy peasy. You could do Green's Bakery if you want easy?"

"With like a green rose for a logo? Nah. I'm probably going with Cakes of Clearwater. I need someone to design a logo for me though. You know anyone?"

"I do, in fact. Joni's sister, Beth. Do you know her?"

"I have seen her a time or two. I think the last time was at your housewarming party. Doesn't Joni have a couple of sisters?"

"Yeah, Beth lives with her and does stuff on the computer. No one knows exactly what all she does, but apparently she's a whiz at it. The other sister is off to vet school in Chicago."

"And Beth does logos? I thought she worked for an insurance company or something."

"She does that, too, or something like that, but Lucy got to talking to her once and found out she also does things like designing brochures and logos and things. I've used her a couple of times to help promote charity events," Ellie said.

Jordyn shook her head. Her friend Ellie had always been neck-deep in good causes. Ellie made her tired, often, and while she admired her ambition and drive, she had no idea how laid-back Mike kept up with her.

"Can you text me her number? I'll give her a call tonight." Jordyn felt a bit of excitement instead of feeling overwhelmed. Maybe things would come together before November first? She'd given her two-week notice to the three people she worked for today. She'd been their private chef for over a year and a half now, going to each of their houses twice a week and making them all three meals each time. One for that night and two more to put together later in the week. That had her making six different meals a day, in two different kitchens, three days a week, Tuesday, Wednesday and Thursdays. Then she did catering for events Fridays, Saturdays and Sundays. Usually she was off on Mondays, but sometimes that didn't work out for her. She would be very happy to work regular hours in one spot instead of running from place to place. To be working in her kitchen that would be laid out just the way she wanted instead of learning on the fly in other people's houses and kitchens and often having to make do because she didn't have what she needed.

Jordyn pulled into her small one-bedroom apartment in the not so good part of town. Her car was ten years old and her apartment rent was cheap and that was why she could save as much as she did. She wore the same clothes almost every day, calling the jeans and the light blue shirt she wore her work uniform. She had four pairs of each, and then a pair of black pants and a khaki-colored pair and about half a dozen shirts that rarely got worn. She wasn't a clothes horse and saving for this bakery had first priority in her life. Now, finally, it was coming true.

She would have regular hours, be closed on Sunday, maybe, so would have a regular day off every week, at least to start, till she got some good people hired. Wouldn't be working evenings unless she chose to cater for someone but she was hoping the bakery would bring in enough soon that she would only have to work there. One job, she marveled. Who would have thought it was finally happening? Not her. But she was ready. Jordyn loved Clearwater and other than being gone for a couple of years for culinary school, had always lived here. It was one of those towns you just never wanted to leave. Or at least she didn't want to.

Most of the friends she had grown up with had drifted back to town after college, and some had never left town for college. Their town had a very nice, very exclusive private college at the edge of town. Out of reach for most of the families but people came from all over to attend. She had taught classes out there at one point, but when she decided that the bakery was her passion, stopped doing that to do the better paying private chef and catering things. Concentrating on saving for her business had been her priority.

Getting out of her car, she walked up to her apartment door, looking around. Once again, it didn't reflect her. Second hand couch, small TV and a coffee table. Her kitchen was sub-par at best. But, she spent enough time in other people's kitchens she rarely cooked at home. When she got her kitchen in her bakery, she'd been toying with the idea of starting a vlog. Why not? It could be fun! She'd thought about it for a while, but didn't have any place to film one. She'd be baking anyway, in her fancy new kitchen with all new professional appliances, so she might do it.

How was she going to wait till day after tomorrow when she would get to see the plans? Tomorrow would just drag.

Well, she had the appointment with Beth tomorrow, so that meant she needed to think of a name. No pressure!

Her mind drifted to Ben as she unbraided her hair and brushed it out. Safely fantasizing only, she reminded herself. He was gorgeous in a big lumberjack sort of way. Those muscles! They were amazing! His hands were huge. What would he look like shirtless? Was the tattoo on his arm the only one he had, she wondered, dropping her rubber band into the jar on her bathroom sink, then kept brushing her hair. Her long braid was good for work, but she enjoyed the feeling of having it down. It was long, to the middle of her back and her mom thought it wanted cut, badly. Why her hair was anything her mom needed to think about, Jordyn couldn't imagine, but apparently it was a big issue with her. But if she was fussing about her hair, then at least she was still thinking. The Alzheimer's was creeping in on her, as well as the physical things, but she seemed to be doing better under the excellent care in the home she'd picked out to go to right after her diagnosis. She'd had a couple of more years at home before she moved in there, but Jordyn felt better knowing she was cared for and where she wanted to be.

And right on cue, her phone rang. Jordyn rolled her eyes, but picked up. "Good evening, Mom," she said.

"Hello, Jordyn, how are you today?" Her mom had been a powerhouse. She'd married and divorced when Jordyn was very young, and put herself through nursing school. Nurses always had a job, she'd told Jordyn all her life. Her sister, Stephanie, had dutifully gone to nursing school and Jordyn knew she was a disappointment for having no inclination to go that route at all. "Everybody knows how to cook," her mom kept telling her. "It isn't a real career."

"I got a call from Clarice," she started. Jordyn moaned inwardly. Great. "She said you gave notice today! Jordyn, what is wrong with you? That's a nice steady job and she's been good to you!"

"Mom, you know I'm starting the bakery. I can't work at the bakery and for my families. I just don't have that much time. I'm just one person!"

"How do you know you will even make a go of this bakery? I can't believe you sank all your grandmother's money into something like this. Your sister is investing part of hers, saving for her children's college tuition and taking some classes to further her career."

Stephanie, the golden child who never did anything wrong. "Of course, she is, Mom. She's brilliant. Me, I just want to bake my little cakes in a nice little store."

"Anyone can bake a cake, Jordyn! Why would they buy one from you?"

"People don't bake their own wedding cakes, Mom."

"And how often do people get married? Two or three times in their lifetimes? Jordyn, you aren't married, you need a good career, a decent income. You know how you live, in that tiny little almost unfurnished apartment, driving that old car that could break down at any minute. I'm not even going to talk about your wardrobe. You need to think about your future. I was talking to one of my nurses today and they said you weren't too old to go to nursing school. They would even help you apply."

Apparently today was one of her mom's good days, Jordyn thought and at least she didn't say she needed her hair cut this time. This was all old news. The nurses seemed to appreciate the cupcakes and cookies she brought them regularly. She doubted they were really invested in her applying to nursing school.

"Mom, I'm hoping to be open by November first. When it's all done, maybe you'd like to come to my grand opening?" Maybe if she saw it all shiny and new, with a lot of people cheering her on, she'd realize... what? Jordyn wasn't sure what she wanted her to realize. But something. That her career choice was every bit as valid as nursing?

"If I'm feeling okay," her mom said, her voice sounding very weak suddenly. "I am certain Clarice would hire you back if you change your mind."

"I'm sure she would, Mom. I have to go, there's my doorbell," she lied. "Love you, talk later."

Jordyn sighed as she hung up her phone. She really needed to set some boundaries with her mother. Talking to her was not good for her confidence or certainty that what she was doing was right. But it was hard when one day, she was as sharp as she'd ever been, and other days she got her and Stephanie confused and even confused her with her aunt, her mom's sister. She should be grateful that her mom still had good days, mentally. Maybe she'd just be too busy to answer her phone, but then she knew her sister, Stephanie would get all the blow up. Stephanie had her hands full with her job, her toddler twins and her husband who was an adorable goofball, but seemed to need a lot of attention. Stephanie didn't need Mom on her case because of her, especially on her, well, Jordyn didn't know what was worse, her good days or her bad days.

Sighing, she went back to her kitchen. One day she would upgrade to a place with a decent kitchen, but right now, everything went to the bakery. Her bakery. She needed to think of a name before she met with Beth tomorrow. Why did nothing jump out at her? Grabbing some leftover stew, she zapped it in the microwave then sat down in front of the television. Her mind drifted again to the mountain man. She had two more weeks of work, then she'd be in the store full time working alongside him. What could she do? Well, paint and clean, put stuff together Make any decision Miranda allowed her to make. Who knew what else, but surely he would tell her.

She also had to set up her bookkeeping and so many financial details. Luckily, her friend, Mike, who was also Ellie's husband, had set her up with his assistant Bryan. Bryan showed her how to easily navigate the intimidating program she'd bought to do the books. It was quite different than what she was doing now, but he made it seem doable and he was only a phone call away, as he assured her.

Jordyn set her stew bowl on the coffee table and pulled a blanket over herself. Feeling too tired to get up and go to bed, she decided to sleep on the couch in front of the TV. Why not? Tomorrow would be a busy day. Maybe the name of her bakery would come to her in her dreams.

"Hi, Beth," she said as she walked in. "I love your house!"

"Thanks," Beth said. "It was our grandmother's and when Joni and I decided we needed a fresh start, coming here just seemed to be the right thing to do. We've been here almost two years now and we both love it."

"It looks like a grandma's house should," Jordyn said. "Huge front porch with a swing, white picket fence, big rooms with high ceilings. I bet the kitchen is fantastic!"

Beth laughed. "Well, come this way and see!" They walked through the living room lined with bookshelves and into a dining room, then past that to a huge kitchen. "Isn't this a grandma's kitchen?"

"It is. I love it!" It was vintage, yet modern. The stove was an older gas stove, that looked restored, a brand-new fridge and a huge farmer's sink. Cheerful red cushions covered the wooden chairs around the big wooden oak table and red and white checked curtains were on the window. It felt homey and warm and Jordyn loved it.

"Here is my office." Beth led her to a small room off the

kitchen. "It used to be my grandma's sewing room. I can still hear her machine running if I listen hard enough."

Jordyn smiled. "I love that too," she said. "My grandma lived in a condo at the beach in Florida the entire time I knew her. She wasn't a typical snap beans on the front porch type of grandma. More of a play pickle ball and zoom around on her golf cart kind."

"I'm sorry about her passing," Beth said.

"Thank you," Jordyn said.

"Hey, Beth! The contractor is here." She heard Joni call from the other room. "You okay?"

"Jordyn is in here with me," Beth called back, then shrugged her shoulders. "Joni is a bit overprotective of me."

"It's nice to have someone who loves you around," Jordyn said. She liked being alone and on her own, but still… Occasionally… no. Just no, she shook her head.

Beth nodded as she sat down in her chair and motioned to the other one for Jordyn. "It is, but really, it can be a little overwhelming sometimes, all her hovering. We are getting bids to remodel the upstairs bathroom, and I hope he comes up with something good, because right now it's barely tolerable. Okay, let's talk about what you are wanting." Beth pulled a computer program up.

Jordyn sighed. "I've got a couple of ideas," she said, "but none are really speaking to me, you know."

"Give me a few," Beth said. "I'll put them in and maybe with a little decoration, one will speak to you. Then we will talk about what kind of sign you want, metal or lighted or just what."

"More decisions," Jordyn moaned, but took a deep breath, "Okay. I've got Clearwater Cakes, Cake & Bake, Rose's Bakery, Rose's Cakes."

"Is Rose your grandma's name?" Beth asked as she typed.

"Yeah, and I'd like to honor her somehow in the name.

Then there is A Piece of Cake, Sunrise Bakery because I plan to open early for coffee and donuts for the people who work downtown. Cake O'clock. See, they are all good names, but really, nothing very exciting."

Beth nodded and worked a little more on her computer program while they talked and she did some kind of computer magic. Half an hour later, they both heard voices in the kitchen.

"Beth, Jordyn, come on. I have tea and cookies and want to show you the bathroom plans," Joni called out.

"We can take a break for a minute, let some of the ideas soak in," Beth said, swiveling in her chair. "I've been smelling those cookies for the last hour."

Jordyn followed Beth back into the pretty kitchen and stopped in the door. Why did her heart skip a few beats and her breath catch? Just because he was so big and so unexpected. She swallowed hard and said as lightly as she could muster, "Why, Ben, are you cheating on me?"

He stood up as they walked into the room and Joni looked at her, surprised.

"No, ma'am, Miss Jordyn. I'm perfectly capable of renovating a bathroom and shop at the same time."

"Are you sure?" she tried to act sassy to cover her surprise. "I didn't think males could multitask."

"I'm one of the few who can," he said and she laughed.

"We'll see about that," she said. "Ben is the contractor on the shop," she told Joni and Beth.

"We figured that out," Joni said. "But right now he's mine."

"I'm not charging by the hour, especially if I get cookies," Ben said, and Jordyn watched him as she took a bite out of her cookie.

"Joni, this is amazing," Jordyn said. "If you want to make these for the shop, I'd love to have them."

Joni smiled. "Well, maybe during the summer or school vacations. Or I could give you the recipe and you could make them. Just call them Grandma Daisy's Oatmeal Cookies."

"I'd love that," Jordyn said. "A whole bunch of my recipes are from family members and old cook books and I think it's great to give them names after the people who made them. Kind of honoring them."

"Isn't your wedding cake recipe from your aunt?"

Jordyn nodded. "And I've collected cookbooks over the years. My favorites are the little ones the Home Extensions or churches put out with people's notes in them."

"Your place is going to be so great," Beth said. "Think of all the new generations who wouldn't get to try them, or even know about those old recipes if it weren't for you, and all the new traditions you'll be starting."

Ben looked at them, and said slowly, "You know what you are doing, don't you, Jordyn?"

She looked at him, puzzled. "What?"

"You are baking memories. If that isn't a name for a shop, I don't know what is."

"Baking Memories," Jordyn said. "Beth, what do you think?"

"I think I love it," Beth said, standing up. "And then we could maybe put little roses over the i's in both words for your grandma, or a larger one underneath or well, come on, let's go design."

Without thinking, Jordyn got up and impulsively hugged Ben. "Such a great idea, thank you!" She rushed out of the room after Beth, totally ignoring her physical reaction to him and how she felt when he hugged her back.

Baking Memories. That was it. It just felt right. Weirdly, just like Ben.

Chapter 2

"I'm sorry," Jordyn said, so frustrated she could barely stop herself from kicking the wall. It was brick. It would hurt, she reminded herself. "I know you two are a thing, but she is making me insane!"

Crossing her arms, she walked to the front window to look at the landscape. There would be a small fair over on the square this weekend. It was a before school started celebration helping to fill backpacks for kids in need, and a food drive for Carol's Hope, a local charity who did a food bank, clothing options, gave out job opportunities, helped people find housing and so much more. Ellie was organizing it, of course, and Jordyn's contribution was donating cupcakes and judging a kid's baking competition.

She felt Ben move behind her. Yes, the tension and stress she felt was not helped by his almost constant presence in her soon to be shop. She tried, she really did, to make him fantasy only, but, well, her body and mind wanted a little more of the giant lumberjack. It wasn't right and she knew it.

"She makes me insane all the time," he said. "Jordyn, look at me."

Slowly, she turned around, flipping her braid over her shoulder. "What? Don't tell me all her good traits. I'm not in the mood after, well, after that!" She motioned toward the small room where she envisioned a cozy little spot for cake tastings and small bridal showers. "We have a totally different vision for that room. I love what she has done with the other rooms but, that one? We just can't seem to come to a consensus. And she makes me feel so, well, less than."

"Jordyn," he said, softly. "That's my sister you are talking about. I know how she is more than you can imagine. You have to let her not get to you."

"Your sister?" Her mouth dropped open. "I thought you were, well, together. You don't look anything alike!" They didn't. Miranda was tall, like Ben but small boned, elegant. He was, well, lumberjack all the way. Sure, she'd hoped they were siblings, but it had been hard to tell. Their hair wasn't even similar. But then, as she knew, like her friend Lucy often did, hair color could easily be changed.

"Genetics are funny, aren't they?" he said. "She's technically my half-sister. My mom died when I was young and I never knew her. Her mom is the only mom I remember," he said. "And really Miranda has a very good heart, she just hides it well for some reason. She's done a lot for me," he continued. "But even I know if someone pulled that stick out of her butt and gave her a good ass whopping, she'd be a lot easier to be around."

Jordyn couldn't help her giggles. "I'd give anything to see that," she confessed. "Okay, I'll listen to her idea again and see if we can compromise. I just think cozy tea room, as opposed to sleekly modern room, fits my theme and this place better."

"This is your dream," he reminded her. "You get final say on things."

"Someone needs to tell Miranda that." Jordyn sighed as she looked around. "Are you going to the event tomorrow in the park?" she asked him. "There are going to be a lot of fun craft booths and food trucks and things. I'm doing cupcakes for sale and for a prize for one of Ellie's games."

"Are you inviting me on a date, Miss Jordyn?" He looked at her and smiled and her breath caught. No. She hadn't been, just making conversation. However, why not?

"I certainly was," she said boldly, but smiled to let him know she was kidding, she hoped, anyway. "At least a casual walk through the park with me. You can help carry cupcakes." Why did she feel like passing out? She'd never invited a guy out before!

"I'm more of a traditional man," he said slowly. What did that even mean? "But I'd love to go walking through the park with you tomorrow. I'll be working here till noon, if you don't mind meeting me here?"

Jordyn laughed. "I'll be here too, for a while, then I'm judging some of the kids' baking, apparently, early. After that, I'll be here to meet with Miranda again and see if we can hammer this out."

Did she really have a date with him? She'd gone from thinking he was totally off limits and questioning his taste in women, to having a date with him in about five minutes. He must think she was really desperate. Flipping her braid back over her shoulder, she tried not to blush as she gathered her things to go. She was going over to Lucy's to bake her cupcakes because, apparently, the bakery didn't have a decent enough kitchen to make the quantity needed for tomorrow. Soon, though, she looked around, she would have the best kitchen in the entire town of Clearwater.

"So are we on schedule?" she asked Ben, trying to pretend that conversation never took place, except that it did and they were going on a date tomorrow.

He nodded. "So far, we might even be a smidge ahead of

schedule, but don't you worry, something will come up that will put us behind. It's how things go."

Jordyn smiled. "Way to be positive," she said. "How's the bathroom going at Joni and Beth's house?"

"A little slow," he said. "Seems Beth is uncomfortable with workers in the house unless Joni is home. Beth works from home during the day, so she can't leave, so we can't work till after school is out. Unless Beth has a friend come over. I don't know what's with her, but I feel badly for her. But it will get done."

"How many projects are you working on right now?" she asked him. He seemed to be here all the time. Well, most of the time.

"This is my biggest one," he said. "But then there are a few other smaller ones, bathrooms, an office building, and Miranda is always working on getting a few more jobs. I just moved to town and am still building my team, remember?"

She hadn't thought about that. "Why did you move here?" she asked. "Just for Miranda?"

"Not just for Miranda. I'm about done for the day here," he said. "I'll see you either in the morning or at noon for our date."

Not a date! It was just a walk around the park! She wanted to say, but managed to hold her tongue. "See you tomorrow," she said as he finished up and walked out the door, giving her a little wave. He obviously didn't want to tell her why he moved to town. If Miranda was approachable at all, she'd ask her. But right now, she was mad at Miranda. No, she wasn't mad, they were only having a professional difference of opinion. It happened. At the end of the day, while she was paying Miranda for her expertise, knowledge and skill, it was still her bakery. If she wanted a cozy, Grandma-inspired room instead of Miranda's vision of a sleek modern area, then cozy it was going to be.

Sleek and modern was excellent in her kitchen. The rest of it would be warm and welcoming and inviting. She wanted people to feel as if they were coming into Grandma's place. Baking Memories. From the memorable wedding cake, to the cookies for the holidays and the cupcakes for a kid's birthday party, and even the morning coffee and donut people looked forward to before work. That was what she was doing. Creating memories for people. She loved the name, and her little shop. She'd be here full time soon. But right now, she had to go make cupcakes for Ellie for tomorrow.

Texting Lucy, *'I'm on my way,'* she packed up and headed over.

"It smells good in here." Max walked into the house. "Hey, Lucy, I'm home. Hi, Jordyn, are those for me?"

"A few are, in rent payment for use of your oven and space," she said. "How was work?" She watched, a little envious, as Lucy rushed into his arms, and he kissed her. Newlyweds. What were you going to do? Just endure it till the new wore off, she guessed.

"Work was great, as always. How are the renovations going? Miranda behaving?"

"Miranda? Too funny. I did find out that the contractor is her brother. Have you met him yet? He seems to be a great guy, very unlike his sister."

"Ben? I didn't know Ben was in town. When did that happen?" Max acted as if he were thrilled. Not.

"Yeah, Ben. How do you know him?" Here she thought Ben was new to town and the area.

"He went to college with us. He's nothing like Miranda," Max said. "We used to, well, we used to hang out together."

Together where? Jordyn wondered. Why did she wonder

where? Probably the bars and frat houses like most college kids. Somehow, though, the way he said it made her curious.

"He's doing a good job on my shop," Jordyn said. "I'm wondering why he moved to town, though. If it was just because his sister was here? He implied he needed a fresh start."

"Is he alone?" Max asked, taking off his tie and tossing it to Lucy as if they did that every day. "I heard he was married."

Jordyn shrugged, a pang of something that was not jealousy hit her. No reason to be jealous of someone who might or might not exist. "No clue. Honestly, I thought he and Miranda were a thing until I heard they were siblings."

Lucy laughed as she draped Max's tie around her neck. "I wonder if there is any man who could put up with Miranda."

"Oh, I'm sure there is, somewhere," Max said. "I'm going to change and then I want a cupcake."

"What kind do you want, chocolate peanut butter, lemon angel food, or cherry vanilla?"

"Yes, please." He grinned at her.

"You will spoil your dinner," Lucy said.

"It's my dinner to spoil," he said and playfully swatted her bottom. Jordyn could hear her laughing as she bent over to take more cupcakes from the oven. One more batch and she would have them all done. Decorating, packing up, and she'd get out of their hair and let them newlywed all over their evening. Would she ever have that? She'd dated, of course. Most people dated. She even thought there were one or two she might have gotten serious about, especially one. But none of them were what she considered, after a short term, long term material. Besides, she had plans for her life. She wouldn't be, as her part-time assistant Moriah told her once, unequally yoked. Jordyn thought she'd been born with ambition and drive. She knew what she wanted and worked to achieve it.

The man in her life, well, he'd have to be a little more. Just like with her shop, she knew what she wanted in a man.

She thought as she decorated cupcakes, half listening to Lucy and Max chattering, about her dream guy. He'd be big, like Ben. She liked big guys, not only tall, but large. It made her feel safe. Bearded. Bearded was good, with a tattoo, maybe? Or two?

He'd have a quick wit and a sense of humor. Laid back, hardworking and fun to be with. However. There was the big 'however' where most of them fell by the wayside. She needed a wall. Most people wanted to break down walls, but she liked walls. Someone strong enough to lean on when things got tough. Who knew where the line was and kept everyone safely on the proper side of the line. A man who wouldn't give up when things got tough, but would do whatever he could to make sure the relationship survived. She'd had wimpy, and ready to give up at the first obstacle. Never again. A rock. A wall. Someone she could push against and know there was no give. In return, she'd be the same for him. A soft place to fall, a best friend, a listening ear and, well, more. Ben fit the physical part, but he seemed almost too easy going. He probably had to be, to counteract his sister growing up. He'd be fun for a few dates, but probably nothing more. Jordyn knew what she needed and wanted and since she was fine alone, there was no need to settle for less.

Not many knew, but she'd been close to being engaged for a very short time in college. She thought she'd found the right one. But instead of the strong alpha male she'd craved and desired, she found she'd hooked up with a bully. She'd learned – online and watching her friends and acquaintances – the difference between being with a bully and being with a strong, dominant male. Never again would she be mistaken.

Just a couple of years ago, all her close friends were single. They all had fun jobs, a place to live and all hung out together often. Now, they were slowly being paired off. Joni was on and off again with Hank, Ellie's brother. Ellie was married to Mike. Lucy married Max who was Mike's best friend and business partner. Bella was dating the dad of one of her clients, but no one thought it would last. Lucy's little sister Moriah was serial dating much to Lucy's chagrin. Izzy and Shana were single as far as she knew, though, which made her feel better. Some. But she was starting to feel the need to have someone. Not just any someone, but her someone. One day, she told herself, placing the last decorated cupcakes in their boxes, then making a small plate to leave for Max and Lucy. Right now she had a shop to open and that was her priority. Once life settled down a little, she could think about dating.

If Ellie, who had the busiest schedule in the world, could find a man, then she could. When she was ready, which she wasn't. She had a bakery to open.

Max helped her carry the boxes to the car before she left. "You be careful around Ben," he warned her, once they were alone outside.

Jordyn flipped her braid back over her shoulder and said, "What?" No one knew she was going to the charity event tomorrow with him. Just two colleagues grabbing lunch and wandering around.

"You heard me," he said very firmly and Jordyn felt a little taken aback. Max had never talked to her like that before. She didn't even know he could. "Ben isn't the gentle giant you think he is. That's all I'm saying, but I hope you understand."

He turned and went back to the house while she stared. No. She did not understand. How could she when he didn't say anything? Men. They were not easily understood. Unlike women. Women used real words and real feelings and made perfect sense. Men were all cryptic and weird. What did he think Ben was or would do or, well, did it matter? Probably Max was just being overprotective. How could he be overprotective when he didn't even know she had a non-date with him tomorrow? Her head spun as she drove home.

Ben watched as they walked toward him. Interesting. How had they found him? He picked up his coffee cup and took a slow sip as they sat across from him. "Mike. Max," he said, putting his cup on the table. "Long time."

"Sure has been," Mike said. "Just heard you moved to town. What happened?"

"Wanted a fresh start," Ben said. "So, you just happen to frequent this place?"

"Yeah, we like Debbie's Diner, we come here for breakfast often," Max said. "Heard you might be here."

"Miranda?" he guessed.

"The one and only," Mike said. "So how is life going?"

"It is going well. How is yours? Heard you both took the plunge."

"Heard you did, too. Laura, I assume?" Mike said. They both ordered coffee and an omelet, so he assumed they planned to be here a while. Fun times.

He picked up his toast and took a bite while looking at them. "It didn't work out," he said shortly. None of their business. What did they want? They hadn't left on a good note, which was mostly Miranda's fault. Why had she decided on Clearwater to settle down in? Did it have anything to do with Mike? She'd been crazy about him for years and it had been more than a little messy there at the end. Or what he hoped was the end. His name hadn't come up though, since he moved here, so he hoped she was well over him. His prim and proper sister had gone a little wild there for a while. Why was Mike here with his ever-present wing man?

"How can I help you?" he asked, watching the waitress

pour their coffee and motioned for a refill for his. "I assume this isn't a social call."

"You make us sound like henchmen sent from The Godfather," Max said.

Ben didn't fight his smile. "Do I look like I'm afraid of either you or The Godfather?"

"Ben, we are just checking on an old buddy," Mike said. "Heard you were around and thought we'd welcome you to town."

"And?"

"And?" They both asked and he smiled at them again.

"Somehow I am not getting the 'hey, it's our old college buddy, let's buy him breakfast' vibe from you."

Mike sighed. "We have settled down," he said.

"Congratulations?" Ben asked and put some of the best loaded hash brown casserole he'd ever had in his mouth. He'd have to compliment the chef.

"We were wondering about you."

"I can't see that is any of your business," Ben said.

"It is if you start dating our wives' friends," Max said.

"I've never done anything that wasn't consensual," he said, putting down his fork and staring at Mike. "Unlike other people."

"Your sister has needed a good butt whipping for years," Max said. "A few more wouldn't hurt her either."

"Not the point," Ben said, standing up. "Appreciate you buying me breakfast. Good to see you both again. I'm sure we will run into each other soon. I'm off to work."

He tipped the waitress a five as he walked out the door and headed over to where he'd left his truck. It was only a block to Jordyn's shop, he'd walk after he grabbed his tool belt. He'd left most of his tools there overnight, but his toolbelt went home with him. Never knew when it would come in handy.

Contemplating his options, he decided to be amused by the visit. He hadn't seen either of them since he paid them a call after what he called the Miranda debacle. He had no idea how his sister's mind worked. It was a complicated thing. He also knew how wild and crazy Mike and Max were in college and he'd been right there with them. They said they had settled down and from what he'd heard around town, they owned some kind of investment firm and were doing very well. They'd both gotten married, and were probably worried about their reputations. Now that part amused him. Had they? Or had they found little kinksters like they were? Did it matter? Not really.

He'd changed a lot since Laura. More than anyone, even Miranda, knew. He was no longer the wild and crazy player he used to be. He had changed and change didn't really cover it. There had been a fundamental twist in the way he thought and acted. Even he didn't understand it some of the time. It was certainly nothing he wanted to talk to Mike and his wingman about. Or even could talk to them about, because he didn't understand it himself most of the time. He just knew he didn't want what he used to desire. He wanted something different.

The event, whatever it was, was already setting up in the little park in the middle of the square. It was some charity thing, he knew, but not sure who for or what it was about. It didn't really matter, most causes were good. He had his own charities he donated to regularly, but realized that others were needed also. There was a lemonade stand, and he could already smell some kind of smoked beef cooking. He knew what he was having for lunch.

Putting the key into the lock, he noticed it was already unlocked. Jordyn must be here already. He thought she had something to do this morning. "Jordyn," he called out. "I'm here."

"In the office," she called back. He walked back that way to say hello and saw her sitting on the floor surrounded by piles of what looked like a deconstructed shelving unit.

He tried not to laugh. She looked so adorably frustrated. "What are you doing?"

"Getting aggravated," she said. "I got a call from the assisted living place at three this morning telling me my mom fell, so I ran out there. They'd gotten her back into bed, so I calmed her down and made sure she was okay. Then I came here because I couldn't sleep and thought I'd try to put this together and just look at it! Who can do this?"

"We can do this," he said, and dropped his tool belt on the floor.

"I should be able to do this!" she said, and put her fist to her mouth as if she were going to cry.

"Hey, we all can't be good at everything," he said as soothingly as he could. "I couldn't bake a cupcake if my life depended on it. Well, maybe I could, but not as good as yours." He skimmed the directions quickly, then tossed them to the side. "Okay, here's what we need to do."

Within half an hour, they had the shelves set up. "Now, where is it going?" he asked her.

"In the pantry," she said. "On the wall without the shelving you are building."

"Why am I not building shelves on that wall instead of buying these?" he asked.

"Don't ask me! I didn't design it, Miranda did and since I already gave her grief over the tasting room, I figured I'd better give in to this one." Her voice kept rising but he couldn't help laughing this time.

"Jordyn, you know she works for you, right? I know she can be overbearing, but if you don't sign that check, she doesn't get paid." He helped her up off the floor and said, "Grab that end."

Overall, he thought, as they moved the shelves where she wanted them, she had been a quick learner and followed directions well. That was a good thing in a woman. He'd turned a little old fashioned in his old age, he told himself, because he had always been attracted to the wild ones. His Laura had been as wild and untamed as they came. Now? He didn't want that anymore. He wasn't that man anymore. Maybe, when he was ready, a woman like Jordyn - sensible, down to earth, hardworking, traditionally female - was what he wanted? He didn't know. He knew he was ready for a new relationship, but he needed to figure out what kind. Yes, he was physically attracted to this dark-haired beauty, but, of course, that wasn't enough. While he might have changed, there were still certain things he needed in a relationship, a partner and a woman. He might look like a big lumbering giant, but his brain was sharp and he knew what made him happy.

He hadn't been happy since Laura. This was a new start in a new town, though, he reminded himself. Things would be different here. "Have you either eaten or had any coffee today?" he asked Jordyn after they settled the shelves into the corner.

"No. I came straight here from my mom's. I do need to get the coffee pot in here, don't I?" She flipped that braid over her shoulder in a movement that enchanted him.

"Come on. I'm buying you breakfast," he said. Second breakfast was a thing. He grabbed her hand and headed back to Debbie's Diner and rather adored the fact she kept her hand in his and followed him without question. "Then you need to get to doing whatever it was you were doing. But, first, sustenance, woman."

He grinned. Although he felt certain Mike and Max had left already, it would have amused him greatly if they'd seen him walk in with one of their wives' friends. Yeah, there was still some crazy college in him, after all.

Jordyn parked her car behind her building, heart pounding. Okay, this would be fun. Why did she feel weird about this morning? It had only been breakfast and he might not even want to eat with her again. She'd been feeling vulnerable and needy. Her sister had her hands full and while she would be there if needed, Jordyn knew she had to be the first call for their mom. That was why she'd stayed in town despite offers from several different places after she graduated culinary school. Her mom had always been there for her and for her sister. She could be here for her in her time of need. Realistically, she was going downhill fairly quickly, but Jordyn didn't want to think about that. No. She would only think of the great care her mom was getting and that she could be there at a moment's notice when needed. Those were good things and her career would be there.

However, this shop, right now, was exactly what she wanted. That could change in a few years, but right now, this felt perfect for her. Her store! It thrilled her to her toes. Not unlike the lumberjack working on her remodel. He'd been so good to her this morning. He'd not laughed – much – at her frustration. She could usually put things together but she'd been upset about her mom and hadn't been able to concentrate. He was a gentle teacher, who didn't get upset with her obvious incompetence that was totally situationally caused. Then, after it was done, he'd taken her out and insisted she refuel with coffee, protein and a big gooey cinnamon bun that might have been almost as good as one of hers. It just made everything better. Then he'd gotten back to work and she'd gone on to judge the kids' baking, and had a great time doing it.

Ben had been beyond kind, though. She couldn't remember the last time anyone had taken care of her. Her mom had been ill for quite a few years now, and looking back, she could see the signs earlier in their lives. No matter how many times she seemed like 'old mom' she was going downhill according to the doctor. Jordyn knew she'd picked up a lot of slack while in high school, then Steph had gone off to nursing school and she went to culinary school and every time they came home for a visit, they could see the decline. Her mom had actually had an uptick in her health for about six months in the home, with their excellent care, nutrition and therapy, but then had started declining again. Now she was in a holding pattern, though recently, she'd started falling too often. They took care but accidents happened. Some days she was like she had been when Jordyn was younger, scolding her about her hair and jobs. Some days she thought Jordyn was one of the nurses or a stranger or her sister. Trying not to take it personally, it still hurt, still made her feel badly. The fact there was nothing she could do but what she was doing, made it worse.

She had felt oddly cherished over the smallness of what any friend would do for a friend. Now it was her turn to take him out to the park and show him a good time. She hoped he liked lemonade shakeups because she'd been craving one all morning.

Unlocking her back door, she smiled. Her back door. Walking down the short hall, she saw the small tip out, now a room that Miranda had convinced her should be an employee's only powder room. She'd figured they would all just use the one out front, but agreed it was a good idea. Much handier, more convenient and private. All those things were good things and really, could you have too many bathrooms? Peeking in there, she smiled. It looked a little more together than it had yesterday when she'd looked last. She hadn't looked this morning, just tried to put the shelf together and left. While she loved being here, she loved showing up and having things done, too. There was always a surprise.

"Ben?" she called out. Walking through the kitchen, she heard the murmur of voices and the front door close.

He turned and smiled at her. "I just sent the guys to lunch. We have an hour. You ready?"

"I'm excited," she confessed. "It is a gorgeous day out there and it smells so good, doesn't it?"

"Yes, it does," he said, opening the door for her, then closing and locking it behind them. "I've not been to one of these in years."

"What? A little street festival?" she asked. "Well, now that you are in Clearwater, you will find we have a lot of them. Ellie loves to organize them, especially for good causes."

"Ellie is Mike's wife, right?" he asked as they walked to the crosswalk. "I'm trying to figure everyone out."

"Don't sweat it. We all become distinct people at some point. Do you know Mike?"

"We went to college together," he said.

"Oh, but yes, Ellie is Mike's wife and the city manager. Miranda designed their new house, by the way. Organizing things like this, for Ellie, is like doing a puzzle or knitting or watching a ball game is to us normal people. She just loves to do events."

"We all have hobbies," he said.

"What are yours?" she asked curiously, and curiously touched as he took her arm as they crossed the street. She'd only been crossing them since she was six, but still, it felt nice.

"One of the reasons I moved to Clearwater was the lake. I love to fish and go boating. You ever fished?" he asked.

"A couple of times in Scouts," she said. "But not for years."

"We might have to go sometime," he said. "See if you like it or not. Want a lemonade shakeup while we are walking around?"

"You read my mind," she said. Okay, now that was wonderful. "I'm buying."

"Not on my watch," he said calmly as if it were a thing.

"You bought breakfast," she protested.

"Don't fight me on this," he warned. "You won't win."

Jordyn laughed and vowed to make sure he had cupcakes to take home tonight. She had a few left over from her donation to Ellie. The thing about cupcakes was you could never make too many. Cupcakes always found a home. "Yes, sir, thank you, sir," she said as she playfully ran her fingers up his arm. "Never argue with the man with the muscles."

"Smart girl," he said, and ordered them two lemon shakeups. "Just as good as I remembered," he said, after his first sip. "What do we look at first?"

Jordyn found the mountain man very easy to talk to as they wandered around looking at the craft booths and watching the games. He tossed a few balls and won her a small teddy bear. A minute later they heard a little kid crying, and one look was all it took for her to realize he'd be fine with her handing it to the little girl. That was sweet.

"I can win you another one sometime," he told her.

"Or I can win you one," she said. "Oh, look! There's Joni and Hank. Have you met them yet?" Why did she suddenly feel as if he should be, would be, part of their little group sooner rather than later? She couldn't forget he was Miranda's brother though. They all respected Miranda, but, well, she wasn't the hang out in the backyard and drink a beer around the pool type. Her mouth went dry as she thought of Ben at the pool, shirtless. Looking over at him, she let her eyes rake him up and down before turning to Joni and Hank who appeared to be on again this week. No one ever knew.

"Hey," she waved at them. "Having fun?"

"We are!" Joni said. "I just saw Ellie getting ready to start the cake walk and she swears there were some really good cupcakes in there to win. We are just heading over." She looked curiously at Ben. Jordyn wondered what she was thinking and figured she'd get a call later.

"Ben, this is Hank, and you already know Joni," she said. "Ben is helping me remodel my store."

"Ben did the new bathroom upstairs," Joni said.

"The one I said I'd do for you?" Hank looked at her.

"The one you said you'd do a year ago and never had time? Yeah, that's the one."

Hank shook his head and gave her a look that Jordyn was happy wasn't directed at her. "Welcome to town," he said to Ben. "I heard you recently moved here."

"I did. Starting my contracting business here in town if you know of anyone who needs help."

"Sounds like you have a good start," Hank said.

"Glad we ran into you," Joni said, grabbing Hank's hand. "Come on, I want cupcakes for dessert tonight. Let's go play!"

"Guess we are going," Hank said. "See you soon, Ben. Looking forward to seeing Jordyn's finished shop."

"You have a lot of friends," Ben said, as they watched them walk away.

"I've lived here all my life," she said. "Other than a stint at school. How about you? Where did you grow up?"

"Up north," he said. "Suburb of Chicago. Then I moved to Bloomington for school and stayed there after school, until I moved here."

"Bloomington is a nice town," she said. "I've visited there a few times."

"I liked it," he said, then obviously changed the subject.

"Let's go grab a sandwich and watch the kids at the petting zoo."

"Sounds good," she said, more curious than ever about his past. Hmm, a mystery! Like she had time to solve a mystery. She assumed he wasn't married. Had he been? Kids? He'd be a good dad, she could tell already. Why was she so interested? It wasn't just because of those muscles and that tattoo, was it? Well, what if it was? It had been a while!

Jordyn blinked frustrated tears from her eyes, or tried to, because they fell anyway. It was okay. She was alone in the shop, having just sent Miranda out. Miranda who had just given her the bad news that the reno budget had to be upped by close to seven thousand dollars and she acted as if it were no big deal. It was a huge deal! Well, on the shows she watched on TV, people sighed a bit, bit their lips and then said, bravely, "no worries" when confronted with upping the budget. But then, they went in and toured and often bought houses that were beyond their budgets too. Why did they do that? It had always baffled her. Why set a budget if someone could agree to work within it, and then just say, nope! She couldn't price a wedding cake at $500 and then get there and say 'oops, I meant $1500.' No. Just no. No one would put up with it, but apparently in renovating a house or business, anything goes!

That extra outgo meant she had to open by November first or before. Or get another job in the meantime. Maybe she'd been hasty quitting her jobs and not taking anymore catering jobs. Maybe this entire idea was foolish. After all, she could have been a nurse, like her mom wanted her to be.

Also, she and Miranda were still butting heads over the tasting room, and she was tired of it. Yes, she hired her for her design expertise but it was her room. Plus she was exhausted and hadn't eaten today. There just hadn't been time. She felt like crawling inside one of her newly installed kitchen cabinets and just bawling. But she couldn't. She had to drive home, make some food, shower the day off her, and then she could go to bed. It seemed like too much right now. She needed some food in her new, almost but not quite there yet kitchen. Well, appliances and countertops and utensils and Jordyn blinked back tears again. It was overwhelming right now. She needed to make sure she ate and slept from here on out. And cut her time with Miranda down. Way down.

She turned all the lights off and then slumped down in her not very comfy folding chair, trying to regroup before she drove home. Jordyn knew she could call any of her friends if she needed someone, but she didn't want to talk to anyone. What she wanted, and not for the first time, was what Ellie and Lucy had. Someone to just go home to. Someone who loved her, and warm and comfortable to be with. A rock she could lean on, and a smile he'd give just for her. To just be there and give her a shoulder to cry on and hold her, and then well, a few other things she didn't want to think about right now. She just needed, no. She didn't need it. She was her own strength. She might want it, but she did not need it. Like she didn't need Miranda telling her that the sleek, modern, sterile cake tasting room would be a wonderful compliment to the showroom that also seemed a little more sterile than she wanted. However, that was practical. It was a showroom, where cakes and other bakery items would be showcased. Where people would be picking up their orders, and coming in from the outside weather, often wearing boots and coats, things couldn't be too close together. Where there would be a few small tables for coffee and muffins, and thus needed to be easily cleaned.

The tasting room, she wanted to be warm and cozy,

one large table with softer chairs, and easy to access. A place where small groups would gather for luncheons or showers or birthdays, and had a good background for the inevitable pictures people were always taking, like a state-ment wall of some kind. A place to linger. The modern layout Miranda had designed looked nothing like her vision. And the furniture needed to be ordered like this week. Miranda had the big discount but if she refused – refused! – to order it, she'd get it and pay the extra. Once again, she thought of the extra seven thousand dollars Miranda said they needed for the exhaust system required by the government who wanted to keep them 'safe' appar-ently. She had the money for the reno, and to hold her a few months before the bakery started making money, and that was going to put a big hit on it. She might have to go back to work, she thought again, and she could, of course, if she had to.

Jordyn allowed a few tears to streak down her cheeks while she tried to work up the energy to go home. She couldn't sit here all night. Maybe she'd see how much renovating the attic space would cost for a small apartment and she could just live here. She knew other people did that. She'd been in a few of their apartments over their shops. It was a wise idea. Or was it? She'd never get a day off if she did that. Besides, now she had to fork over more money for the reno she was doing now. Stupid code. Who made up this rule everything had to be to code? Well, it wasn't Miranda so she needed to stop being aggravated with her.

Shifting in her chair, she saw a shadow outside her door and her heart pounded, but then she recognized the silhouette. Her – no, not her – the mountain man standing outside her door.

For some reason she wanted to go hide, and not let him know she was there or that she was crying. But it was too late.

He was already inside and striding across the floor toward the kitchen when he stopped.

"Jordyn? You okay?" he asked. "Didn't mean to scare you. I left my phone in the kitchen and since I was having dinner at the diner, thought I'd run by and get it before I went home." He paused. "You okay? Why are you sitting here in the dark?"

"I was just dreaming," she said, trying to sound light and happy. "Just a little down time before I headed home."

He pulled up a chair and sat down next to her in the dark. "Or you could tell me the truth," he said in a tone she didn't think sounded like a suggestion. How had he known?

"Your sister," she started.

He laughed that low Ben chuckle she had come to appreciate and enjoy too much. "I get it. Miranda means well, she just doesn't have much of a bedside manner," he said.

"Or one at all. But to be fair, it isn't really her fault. She and I simply have different visions of the side room, and then she hit me with a big bill for, of all things, an upgraded exhaust system. Apparently the rules recently changed and the one we thought we were doing won't be up to code. And then there is all the stuff I have yet to order, and–" she stopped. He didn't need to hear all her problems. He'd be worried about his paycheck. What was wrong with her? She sniffled, blinked hard, and bit the inside of her cheek not to full on sob. "I'm sorry. I'm overtired and hungry."

"When did you eat last?" He stood up and strode into the kitchen in the dark. She thought at first that he was going to make her something in her empty kitchen, but remembered he'd left his phone in there. He was probably tired too. He'd worked all day, also. At least he'd had supper though.

Slowly, Jordyn got to her feet, and gathered her stuff. She needed to go home. "Thank you for listening to me," she told him when he came back. "I guess I needed an ear. I'm going to head home now."

"No, you aren't," he said as if it were a thing.

"Excuse me?"

"You are getting in my truck and we are getting you some food."

"Oh, you don't have to do that," she protested, although really, just sitting back for a minute and letting someone take charge and feed her sounded beyond lovely. Just for a little bit. Food and sleep and she'd be back to herself in the morning. Maybe even strong enough to stand up to Miranda. She'd better eat her spinach if she wanted to be that strong.

"Wasn't asking you," he said, taking her hand. "I was telling you. No way am I letting you drive in your condition. I've lived with women. Rule number one is don't let them get hangry."

"Hangry?" She almost laughed. It was an odd word for a lumberjack to say.

"Yes. Come on." He reached over and swatted her bottom, making her jump a little. "Don't argue or I'll have to paddle that cute little butt."

He thought her butt was cute? He swatted her? Paddle? Why wasn't she outraged instead of oddly, well, comforted? "Yes, Sir," she said. "Or do I mean, No, Sir?"

"You just climb in the truck and don't think about it," he said. "I got this."

He had this. Yeah. That's what she wanted to hear right now and once again, the tears started to flow.

Chapter 3

Ben sighed and walked back to the little room Jordyn called the tasting room. They were in there butting heads. Nothing was getting done, accomplished or decided. They were simply bickering and while he was out here installing the display cabinets in the big room, he'd heard all he wanted. Fine. He knew how to handle bickering children. The rest of his crew were finishing up the bathroom over at Joni and Beth's and then would be here for the final push to get this place done. But they seemed stalled on this little room and he was done with it.

He let his big frame fill the doorway and waited till they both stopped talking and looked at him. "I've had all of this nonsense I can take," he said slowly, and watched Miranda's brain scramble to form her argument. "No." He held his hand up at her while Jordyn just stared at him, astonished. He couldn't blame her. This was her shop, after all, Miranda was the designer and he was only the worker boy. Well, worker boy was about to put his size fourteen boot down.

"Ben," Jordyn started and he pointed at her.

"Quiet now. I've listened to you both all morning and

nothing is getting done, I'm sick of it. Before you two leave this room, things will be decided. Do you understand me?" They both stared at him as if he'd grown two heads.

Fine, the big guns. "I swear, if I have to put you both over my knee, paddle you till you bawl, and then stand you in the corner, I will do it. Tell her, Miranda."

"I don't know how Laura put up with you," Miranda said. That was mean, he thought but put that to the side. But she said to Jordyn, "We better figure something out."

"Sit." He pointed to the two folding chairs in the room. "Now. Unless you want to be sitting on sore butts." His proper little sister scrambled to her seat, but Jordyn moved a little more slowly. She was going to have to be taught he meant what he said, but he hoped not to have to do it in front of Miranda today. "Now," he told her. She sat, her dark eyes huge, looking at him in, well, he couldn't tell what. Who knew what went on in a female's brain?

"Now. What is the worst possible outcome here? Jordyn, you first."

"Worst? I will hate it, it will cost me a bunch of money, and then I'll have to redo it and lose business."

"Miranda?"

"It won't be to code, it won't reflect who I am as a designer, people will hate it, and Jordyn will be unhappy with my work."

"What did you hear, Jordyn?"

"She's worried about the code, which I appreciate, and that she's worried more about her reputation than about what I want."

"That's fair," Miranda said. "And yes, I don't want people to come in here and see shabby chic and farmhouse, and over-stuffed sofas that are going to get filthy in two weeks, and chintz on the windows, and pictures of cows on the wall and think that is what I do."

"Is that what you think I want?" Jordyn sounded aston-ished and Ben smiled. Now they were getting somewhere.

"Yes!" Miranda said. "Yes. That is what you've been telling me you want and I just don't see the vision!"

"I don't see that vision either," Jordyn said. "I was thinking more of big, well, yes, farmhouse table. You know, long and maybe oak or cherry, one that warms the room and feels welcoming to gather around, with some kind of comfy chairs around it, but not chintz or overstuffed, easy to clean but soft. Maybe a bench against that wall, with a small table over there to hold gifts, a place to take pictures, like a statement wall, but no, not cows, and–"

Miranda interrupted her, "Now this I understand." She got out her ever-present notebook and started drawing while Jordyn scooted closer to her. Ben folded his arms. Finally. They had both been so stubborn about being right, neither of them had been listening to the other. All it had taken was a threat of a good paddling and a couple of leading questions. Who said women were complicated?

He left the room and went back to installing the display case.

After he left, but before the power tools started up again, he heard Jordyn ask softly, "Did he mean that?"

Miranda spoke quietly too. "About the spanking? Oh, yeah. Ben never says anything he doesn't mean." Then resuming her normal voice, asked, "So what is your vision for the windows?"

He smiled as he went back to work. That was handled well. He thought back to Laura. He'd spanked her often, before and after their marriage. Mostly they were fun, before sex foreplay kinds, but occasionally, she'd needed a thorough butt reddening, leg kicking, bawling, squalling, begging, very thorough paddling. He could always tell when she was building up to one. Sometimes he let her build and sometimes he just nipped it in the bud. Both ways satisfied them both. Well, at the end.

He remembered as he worked.

His little blonde angel was in one of her moods. He could tell as he walked in from fishing. "What's the matter, Butterfly? You have a hard day at work?"

"No. I did not," she snapped at him, then relented. "Catch anything? Making me fish for supper?"

"Yes, ma'am. I did and I will." He kicked his boots off and put his gear down. "So what's your deal?"

"I don't have a deal." She stomped around barefoot in the kitchen wearing those adorably too short shorts and a tiny tank top. Yeah. His wife was hot. "I'm allowed to not be all roses and sunshine all the time!" Her voice rose with every syllable and he just looked at her. Something was wrong, but he knew how to make it right. The only question was to blister her rear before or after he took a shower. He could do it now and then demand she join him in the shower and wash his back, or he could wait and smell a little better. Hell, his back needed washed. He'd just do it now, and then they could have a hot shower, a good afternoon and evening together. She only worked till noon on Saturday, so hadn't been home long. Long enough to change and work herself into a mood. Well, technically, she'd been working up to it for a couple of days now. Time to get it settled. He wanted to have a fun weekend, not one where he was retreating to the TV in the basement to watch the game and get away from her.

"Want to talk about it?" he asked, but already knowing the answer.

"There is nothing to talk about." And with that, she

slammed her glass down on the counter and started to dramatically sweep out of the room.

"Bring the paddle on your way back," he told her, then grinned and stroked his beard as he watched her stop mid-step. She'd heard him. He reached down, pulled the fish out and put them on the cutting board he saved for cleaning fish. He had the first one almost done before she walked back in the kitchen.

He just pointed to a spot on the counter and she reluctantly put the paddle he'd upgraded to a while back on that spot.

"Go stand in that corner till you are ready to tell me what's wrong," he said. "Then after your paddling, we can take a shower."

"I've already showered today," she grumbled.

"Corner," he said. He'd only caught two fish so it wouldn't take him long to clean them. Then he'd stick them in the fridge with a little lemon and pepper while he took care of business.

Washing his hands a few minutes later, he looked over where she stood squirming in the corner. "Hold still," he told her. "Unless you are ready to talk."

"Ben," she whined. He ignored her while he filled a glass with some lemonade she'd made earlier, apparently, because it wasn't there when he left this morning. That was nice of her. Maybe he'd go easy on her to say thank you. No, that wouldn't satisfy either him or his little masochist who swore she wasn't, but sometimes just needed her pain. And his dominance. He could flex those muscles for his little butterfly if she needed him to and apparently today, she did.

"You ready?" he said. She shook her blonde curls and her hands went to cover her shorts covered bottom. "Move your hands and start running your mouth."

She folded her arms across her back above her bottom and

he regretted he hadn't told her to lose the pants. Soon. Taking another sip of lemonade, he sat down on the high bar stool with the paddle within reach and waited.

"My car is making a funny noise," she said. Ben tried not to laugh. Yeah, that wasn't it.

"Huh. Wonder what we should do about that?" he said.

"I don't know. I don't care!"

"But I do," he said. "And there are people out there who actually fix cars for a living, if it's above my paygrade. So what is really wrong?"

"Nothing." She tightened her fingers on her arms, he noted.

"Well, there's a few extra for lying. Better start talking, because we have a long weekend and you might want to sit at work come Monday morning."

"I don't want to go to work Monday," she blurted out. "I want to quit."

"Then quit," he said. "You going to stay home and be my sex slave or what?"

"No, I'm not quitting, I'm just mad and frustrated. I screwed up a big project and it's going to take me weeks to fix it."

"You hate messing things up," he said, slowly. "But in life those things happen."

"I know they do, but I just don't want to deal with it!"

"Part of life," he said. "We all have to do things or go through things we don't want to." How little did he know how those words would haunt him in less than a year when she was going through something no one wanted or expected to go through. Especially not a healthy, strong, twenty-five-year-old. "But right now, get that little butt here over my knee."

"I don't want a spanking," she whined as she didn't move from the corner.

"Good thing because you're getting a paddling. Much more than just a spanking."

"Thanks," she muttered as she started to turn toward him.

"And don't worry, we'll talk more about that issue at work later, after you have a good cry."

"Sweet of you," she'd said, but kept moving toward him. They'd done this dance often enough, he knew she knew her moves. But part of the fun for him was telling her. Having her bend to his will.

He held up his hand when she was halfway across the room. "Drop the pants."

"No." What he wouldn't do to hear that whine again.

"Now." She locked her eyes with his and dropped her pants then kicked them to the side and walked over to him.

"That's right," he told her, sitting up in the stool and patting his knee. "Get that little butt over here so I can make it nice and red for you."

"Ben," she whined again, as she just simply did what she was told. Would he ever find that again?

He could still feel her warm body draped over his lap, see her sweet bottom wriggling while she tried to get adjusted.

If he could have a do over, would he pick that paddle up again? Of course he would. He loved her and would do anything for her, and turning that little bottom red was exactly what she both wanted and needed.

He picked up that paddle again in his mind and cracked it down on her bare little bottom and heard her perfect voice as she yelped.

"I'm sorry you had a bad day," he said, as he brought it down twice more. "But that is no excuse for you to get all stressed out." He knew what his little butterfly wanted and proceeded to deliver it, despite her squeals, protests, leg kicking and eventual sobs. Watching that gorgeous butt turn from pale white to pink to bright splotchy red while it wiggled and tightened and clenched never ceased to fascinate him. Hearing her squeals and howls and pleas and almost being able to feel her attitude change captivated him. Everything about her was enchanting, even her little pouty foot stomp when she needed a good spanking enchanted him. What he wouldn't give to see that again.

Once it was over, when he could tell her attitude had changed and she was ready, she crawled on his lap, and hugged his neck while sobbing and he patted her back and inhaled her scent. He could still smell it. The sweet scent of a little stress sweat, tears and vanilla and something that was simply her. He'd slept with her nightgown for over a year after she passed.

Then he thought of Jordyn. Could she be his chapter two? Was he ready for one, finally? How would he have to adapt? He and Laura had fit like two spoons. Change would be challenging. However, he smiled as he heard her and his sister's voices in the other room, he thought he could manage a little change. Besides, his paddling hand was getting itchy. Someone needed to go over his knee and soon.

"Are you nervous?" Ben asked.

Jordyn climbed into the truck while he held the door open. "A little, I guess," she said. "How did you know?"

He got in on the other side and said, "You have tells."

"I don't have tells! What are they?" She fastened her seatbelt and looked at him.

"That would be telling," he said.

"Ha ha. Are we dating?" she asked, then covered her mouth. She hadn't meant to ask that. What if he said nope, we are just friends? Why had her mouth said that? Nerves? She held her breath. Was she dating this mountain man? Or were they just buddies? Or whatever the term was nowadays?

"Dating?" he said and Jordyn thought he looked a little shocked or surprised. Then he said, slowly, as he maneuvered out into the street. "Jordyn, I haven't dated since Laura."

Okay, then.

"How long has it been since your divorce?" she asked.

He didn't look at her but she noticed his fingers gripping the truck's steering wheel tighter. "We aren't divorced."

"Yet?" she asked. No. She would not, could not date a married man. Why hadn't he told her this before?

Ben shook his head. "Laura died."

"Oh, Ben. I'm so so sorry. I had no idea. What happened?" Jordyn felt horrible. What did you do or say?

"Cancer," he said. "It was rough and it was fast. She's been gone just over three years now. It was hard. She was... everything. She even liked Miranda and we know how challenging that can be."

"She sounds impressive," Jordyn's mind raced. Ugh. This was a game changer. She'd thought Ben had been divorced a few years and was probably over it. She didn't know anyone who had lost a spouse when they were young. How did you get over that?

"Are you okay to talk about it?" she asked. Was it better to ignore the subject or hammer it all out? Suddenly, she forgot to be nervous about taking him to Ellie's for dinner tonight. Their first outing as a... as a what? That was what she didn't know.

"Sometimes," he said. "Sometimes not. I'm here with you now, though, and doubt you really seriously want to talk about my wife."

"Do you still consider her your wife?" she asked. Hmm, was that normal? She didn't know.

He half shrugged. "Well, I'm not certain what else to call

her. I can't call her my ex, because she isn't. She loved me till the day she died. It seems to bother people when I call her my dead wife. I don't know. What do you think?"

"I don't know, either," she said. "It isn't something that's really come up a lot, I guess. Ellie's folks died in a car accident and she still refers to them as her parents, but that's a little different, I guess."

"Especially if you are out with a gorgeous woman," he agreed. "Who probably doesn't want to talk about your dead wife. Tell me, you been married or engaged or anything?"

Jordyn looked around. "Gorgeous woman? Where? But no. I've been busy. Between work and school and my mom, well, there hasn't been time for many guys. Couple of semi-serious relationships, but nothing recently."

"How's your mom?" he asked.

"She's not well," Jordyn said. "But she has a lot of really good caretakers and is getting the best care we could want. Some days are really good and she's the same old pain she's always been and other days she doesn't know who I am."

"Is she here in town?" he asked.

Jordyn nodded and pushed her hair back. Instead of the tight braid she usually wore, she'd brushed it all out and let it fall down her back. She felt like a real woman instead of a working stiff. She changed the subject. "It will be a fun night. You are going to love my friends."

He shot her an odd look, but she continued, "You've met a few of them already. Joni and Hank will be there, you met him at the park a while back. They seem to be together this week, at least. Hank is one of the smartest people you will ever meet, almost as smart as Lucy." Ben had met Lucy and let that one go. She was sweet and cute enough, but smart? Well, what did he know?

"Then of course, Ellie and Mike, because it's their house. She's probably going to try and rope you into helping her with one of her events. Just say yes the first time. She will wear you down anyway."

"I'll remember that," he said.

"Mike's best friend Max will be there, with his wife Lucy. You will love Lucy. Everybody does. Well, except for Mike, but I think by now him thinking Lucy irritates him is more of a habit than anything else."

"I met her at your shop the day I started work," he said. "So you are bringing me into all these established pairs. Couples?"

She couldn't tell if he was teasing her or not. "Just my friends," she said. "I guess we are at an age where people are thinking of settling down."

He didn't say anything. Jordyn bit back a sigh. He'd already done the settling down thing and she felt sure he wasn't ready to do it again. Besides, this was just two friends hanging out, wasn't it? Since he hadn't answered her question, she had to take it as that.

It wasn't like she had any time to date anyone. Once the store opened, she'd be crazy busy, she hoped, plus learning all the stuff she didn't know she had to learn. Luckily, Bryan was helping her set up an easy bookkeeping system. "Oh, Bryan and Alex are going to be there too." She looked over at him. "You will love Bryan. I've never met Alex, though. He works at the hospital. I think he's a doctor but I'm not sure."

He nodded. "You have a lot of friends." he said.

She smiled. "It isn't a big town. Ellie, Lucy and I have been friends forever, and the rest have just connected to us over the years." Would this mountain man be part of their group eventually? She was beginning to hope so. "Bryan and Alex bought a house from Ellie when she was a realtor, and then Bryan was hired at Mike and Max's office when Lucy quit work there."

"You all have your noses pretty far up each other's butts," he said. "Seems like anyway."

"Nah, we don't get together nearly as much as we used to," Jordyn said. "We are all so busy anymore, this is actually a rare treat."

"I'm glad to be invited," he told her. "Is this the road?"

"It is," she said, watching his hands as he turned the truck's steering wheel. "Your sister designed this house, if you didn't know." They were pulling into the large circle drive that Ellie had insisted on. Plenty of room to park.

"Then it will look great, I'm sure," he said. "You happy with how your little room is coming out now?"

She nodded, but then the question she'd been wanting to ask popped out of her mouth, "Would you really have spanked me?"

Ben chuckled that deep sound she enjoyed so much. "You have no idea how tempted I was." He held up two fingers. "You were this close to going over my knee and getting your bottom warmed."

"You can't do that," she told him, ignoring the feelings his words gave her.

"Can too," he said.

"Ben! No! You can't!"

"Why not? I've never seen two people who needed a good blistering more than you two did. You were lucky that just a warning fixed your problem. Next time, you won't be that lucky, I'm sure." He parked the truck and she sat there, almost stunned. What?

"Ben!" she started but then shut her mouth as she got out of the truck. "We can discuss this later."

"You want to talk about me warming that cute little butt of yours later? Yes, ma'am, if you insist." He grabbed her hand as they walked up to the house and gave it a little squeeze. "Let's go have fun with your friends, okay?"

"Okay," she said, not really sure what she was agreeing to – discuss spanking or have fun with her friends, or both? Didn't matter – she loved holding his hand. It made her feel small and as if someone was taking care of her. Realizing it was only a temporary thing made it feel okay. After all, she didn't need someone taking care of her. She was the caretaker. From feeding people, to making their celebrations special with her bakery goods, to caring for her mom and helping her sister out when she could, to lending an ear and advice to her friends, she was the one who did the caregiving. It felt a little nice to feel cared for, even for a minute or two. It wasn't something she should get used to, though, she reminded herself. It was just the proximity thing. They were together so much right now, but once the shop was done, and she was opened, who knew when or if she would see him again? They were simply comfortable together, that was all.

Ben rang the bell and waited for it to be opened, and thought. He hadn't seen Mike or Max since they tried to warn him about, well, about what? Dating Jordyn? Running rampant through town? They'd all been wild and crazy back in college doing things that would make their mamas have heart attacks if they ever found out. He'd met Laura their senior year and that had been it for him. She was everything. Smart, funny, gorgeous and could match his kink with more of her own. She loved to play as much or more than he did. A few months after her death, he went a little wild again. He was over that now, though. Grief did that to you.

Tonight, though, he hoped to make peace with Mike and Max and maybe make a new friend or two. Just have a little fun with Jordyn. If he could do that, it would be a good night. Good nights didn't happen often. Still. But he was ready for one, and for more than one. If he could have one, maybe he'd have a few more? That was why he moved here, right? For a fresh start in a new town, to meet some new people and get back to living. So, even though he was hanging out with some old college buddies tonight, instead of brand-new people, it was still a start.

"Come on in, Jordyn. Hello, Ben." Mike stood in the doorway. Mike was one of the few people Ben knew who could look him straight in the eye. He towered over most people, but while Mike couldn't match his bulk, he was almost as tall.

"Mike," he said, easily. "Nice of you to invite us." Handing him the bottle of wine he'd brought, he waited.

"Welcome to our home," Mike said, though it sounded a little reluctant to him, which made him smile. *Get over yourself,* he thought.

"Thanks, it is a real nice place. I hear my sister had something to do with that."

"Miranda is good at what she does," Mike said. "I'm happy she's doing so well. Who would have thought a designer business was so needed here in Clearwater?"

"You have to find a need and fill it," Ben said. "Miranda does that, despite herself."

Mike laughed. "That's for sure. Come on, we're starting with beer and sodas on the patio."

"Sounds good," he said, wondering where Jordyn went.

Probably the patio, he figured, as he followed Mike out there. The house did look nice, he thought as he walked through it. Warm, inviting, cozy. Everything, he grinned, his little sister wasn't. But apparently she knew what her clients wanted.

They got to the patio, and there was Jordyn with two beers in her hand. "Here you go," she said, handing him one. "Party time! Everyone who hasn't met him, this is Ben. He's Miranda's brother but don't hold that against him. He's also the general contractor working on my shop."

"And he did our bathroom remodel," Joni chimed in.

He shook Hank's hand and then was introduced to Bryan, who said, "My husband couldn't come tonight, got held over for another shift, but happily my sister Jenna is visiting from St. Louis, so I brought her along."

Mike said, "And you know Max, this is his wife, Lucy, and of course, my gorgeous wife, Ellie."

"Good to meet you all," Ben said, settling down next to Jordyn in a surprisingly sturdy chair. His big fear was plastic woven weave lawn chairs. They just weren't up to someone his size. He got comfortable and took a sip of his beer, then listened for a few minutes as the conversation flowed around him.

"So, Jenna, what do you do?" Ellie asked.

The small blonde woman smiled and said, "Right now I'm a hotel manager, but I'm looking to open a BnB somewhere. Bryan was telling me about Clearwater and the gorgeous lakefront and how close the Shawnee National Forest was. I came to do a little recon and see how I feel and if there is anything here next to my favorite brother that I might want to invest in."

"Oh, that sounds wonderful," Ellie said. "A bed and breakfast would be a wonderful addition to the town. I'm a…" She stopped and looked at Mike. "I used to be a realtor, but this one won't let me do it, even part time, anymore."

"On top of your full-time job and all your committees and events and everything else you do? No." Mike lifted his beer. "The Master has spoken."

Ellie pouted his way and Ben chuckled silently. Yeah, he had met Master Mike and if Ellie had, well, she'd be making sure her toes were well off that line. He thought Matt and Max had settled down, though, as he had. Who knew though?

"But I have contacts. When you get serious about looking, let me know and I'll have someone get hold of you and take you to a few promising places," Ellie said.

"Thank you!" Jenna seemed excited and Ben figured Clearwater would have a new BnB sooner than later. Nothing wrong with that. If Miranda designed it, he'd be there working, he figured.

They sat around drinking and talking for the next hour till Ellie announced food. "Food I didn't make?" Jordyn said, seeming offended. "I'm not sure about this!"

"Get over yourself," Ellie told her. "It's your day off. Tell me more about how it is going? Mayor Lydia and I want to be there for your ribbon cutting."

"I'm having a ribbon cutting?" Jordyn asked.

"You are!" Ellie said. "And we will have a big grand opening ceremony and you will do some giveaways and it will be so fun. I need about a two-week lead time to get things set up, though."

"I have to give a two-week notice?" Jordyn seemed nervous or scared or something, he noted. He'd have to find out why later.

Ellie nodded and Lucy laughed. "It isn't that big a deal, Jordyn. Just call me or Lucy and we will set things up. All you have to do is what you do best. Make food."

Jordyn slipped over to him and he pulled her into a side hug. He could feel her trembling. What was going on?

"Let's go eat," he told her, taking her hand, then whispering, "we can critique the food on the ride home if you want."

She giggled, but only half-heartedly. Interesting. Well, he'd find out more later. But for now, he'd just enjoy dinner. Lucy was adorable, he thought, in a flighty air head sort of way. Smart? Well, that's what Jordyn had thought. Max probably had his hands full with her. He had always enjoyed a little bubbly ditzy blonde, but realized how she probably irritated

Mike. Mike wasn't into ditzy or bubbly. Jenna was interesting. Ellie, for all her five foot almost nothing was intimidating and seemed to be the crowd leader while quietly deferring to her husband. Joni was quiet and seemed reserved. She was a school teacher, he'd found out, and was probably fun once you got her loosened up.

The women he liked. Now the men, well, he'd hold his opinion, but had to say Mike bought the good beer, so he wasn't going to complain.

He listened more than he talked, but thought about Jordyn's reaction when he mentioned putting her over his knee. Funny how so many females seemed intrigued by the thought, till it was actually happening. The reality often didn't match the fantasy, but oddly, they would keep coming back for more. Why? He didn't know but was just happy they did. It was a nice warm up to more fun things later, he'd found. Maybe he'd put the dark-haired beauty over his knee tonight, just to see how they both felt about it. Sometimes a fun little spanking, well, fun for him anyway, broke a lot of ice and barriers. Jordyn had some and he felt intrigued to find out why and what they were.

He turned to Bryan and they started talking about the Cubs surprising winning streak. At least he'd found a kindred spirit.

Walking around the backyard later to stretch his legs, he admired the landscaping. That was on his list of things to add to his company. A landscaping service. But while he walked, he thought on all the random connections he'd seen tonight. He was only in Clearwater because of Miranda. Who, he knew, though she denied it, only was here because of Mike. She seemed to be okay now, but he knew she'd gone off the deep end for a while over him. Why? He didn't know. Mike was a decent guy, but there were a lot of decent guys out there. Bryan had only met Ellie when he moved to town with his husband, who transferred here because his folks had once owned a cabin on the lake, and it brought back memories for him. Everyone seemed interwoven in this town. Even him, he guessed.

He walked back to the gazebo where Jordyn stood under what she informed him were fairy lights. "Apparently, I'm now volunteering to help do lights and booths for something called a Weiner dog race," he told her. "And you look gorgeous, by the way."

"It's the lighting." She giggled and flipped her hair back. He adored her hair, even when she wore it in that tight braid, but hanging free like it was today, it was mesmerizing. "And yes, that Weiner dog race and the Christmas parade are two of Ellie's pet projects. Then the little events like the one we went to last week are her idea of fun. Just something to pass the time. I'm working there, too. And probably donating cupcakes or cookies."

"This is real nice," he said, looking around.

"It is," she agreed. "The house is lovely, but this little gazebo is my favorite, especially when they have the lights up. There's a koi pond over there." She pointed and he took the opportunity to take her by the arm. Their first kiss surprised him. Had he been thinking of doing that all night? At first she seemed startled but settled down in his arms, and relaxed into it. Her lips tasted vaguely of the chocolate cake they'd just had. He felt her tense, tremble then relax again. That was a good girl. They fit together very well, he noted while he gently took a handful of her hair and brought her head back further for better access.

"Well," he said, when they finally broke apart. "That was amazing. Are you okay?"

She nodded, and touched her finger to her lips as he reluctantly let go of her. He smoothed her hair. "We better get back to the house," he said. "Before Ellie sends a search party."

"That was... wonderful." Her voice sounded breathy, as if she couldn't catch her breath. That was a good thing. He liked that reaction. But what was he doing? Going too fast. Still, he grabbed her hand as they walked back to the party together. "So tell me about this Weiner dog race."

Jordyn lay in bed later that night, staring at the ceiling. What was it about the big mountain man that intrigued her so much? She'd never kissed a man with a beard before. She liked it, she decided and touched her lips again. It was different, in a very good way. She never felt safer or more scared when she was in his arms. It was odd. Plus he was smart, and funny, and knew how to do stuff. Never underestimate the appeal of a man who knew how to fix things, her Grandma Rose had told her. Grandma would have adored him. Then, too, he was kind, gentle, most of the time. Except when he was threatening to put her over his knee. What was with that? Why did that intrigue her?

It didn't matter why. It just was. What would that be like? She guessed she'd find out. Maybe? She'd be seeing him at her shop tomorrow. Baking Memories. Her sign would be in soon and he'd supervise the hanging of it. Apparently that was part of the sign maker's service, hanging it.

Ellie and Lucy would be planning her grand opening. For some reason that had freaked her out earlier. It made it seem too real and almost frightening, but she didn't know why. This is what she'd planned for and worked for, for years now. The reason she stayed in this small, sparsely furnished apartment and drove her old car. The reason she saved every penny, and it was almost terrifying to see it flying out of her bank account now. It was for a good cause and for good, solid, business reasons, but still, it bothered her. Soon she'd be able to start putting it back in, she reassured herself. That would feel better.

Even though she still considered renovating the upstairs for a small apartment for herself, then she could get rid of the rent on this one altogether, save even more, eventually.

Besides, then Ben would be around longer, and she wouldn't let Miranda anywhere near it. She could design her own place. At least with Ben's help, she could, probably. She'd ask him what he thought in the morning, she decided, and go up there and look around. Something to keep her mind off her opening nerves.

It was still well over a month away. There was no reason to freak out.

Jordyn continued to tell herself that as she walked into the shop in the morning. No reason to freak out. The bathrooms should both be finished this week, so she planned to paint them, and explore the attic. Last time she was up there was right after she bought the place, but if she recalled, it used to be an apartment. The downside to living on site was that she wouldn't ever feel like she got a day off. She'd always be on call, even if she officially had the day off. Jordyn looked around and smiled. She wasn't sure that was a bad thing, now, though a few years down the road it might be. But if so, then she could rent it out and move. See, there was a solution to most things if you thought about it long enough.

She got the paint out, deciding she'd do the small employees only bathroom first. That one she was painting a vibrant blue. The one out front, Miranda had decided needed to be a light gray. At least Miranda was with her on the 'no white' bandwagon. Everything was always white on the TV shows, and she wasn't a fan. Of course, in the kitchen, that was different.

Lucy's house was full of color and life, and she adored Lucy's house. It was small, cozy, and brimming with energy, just like Lucy herself. Ellie's house was warm and inviting, but more formal. What would she do with hers?

She had the small bathroom painted before Ben showed up that morning. "Hey, Jordyn." She heard his rumble from the front door and smiled. She'd miss that when he stopped coming. Immediately, she decided she'd be doing the apartment. Eventually, he'd move onto another project, but she could work him a while longer.

"Morning, Ben," she called, coming out of the kitchen, past the display case and inhaled. "You brought coffee! Thank you!" Taking the offered cup from him, she said, "Want to go upstairs with me?"

"You inviting me to see your etchings, Miss Jordyn?"

"My what?"

He didn't answer her, but opened the side door that entered into the attic. "After you," he said.

"You're just letting me go first in case there are mice up there," she said as she headed up the surprisingly wide stairs.

"How did you guess? There's a light switch at the top of the landing," he said. "Why are you wanting to come up here today?"

"I'm thinking of remodeling this so when my lease comes up, I can move in here."

"I see," he said, moving behind her as her fingers felt for the switch. "Well, let's take a look at it."

They looked around. The large room had three doors off it, and a huge window that overlooked the square. "Nice view," she said.

"Same as in your front shop window, but a little different perspective," he said, standing behind her and looking over her. "Nice."

"I do like our little square." She turned around suddenly and bumped into him. "Oh, sorry, I was going to check out the bathroom."

"Well, it has one," he said. "I looked at it when the plumber and I were going over the place." He didn't move out of her way, and he was too big for her to shove over, so she just stood there a second. Half smiling, she remembered what one of her requirements for a man was. A wall. Here was her wall. She looked up at him, past his chest, to his beard, up to his eyes. There he was. He smiled at her and she tried not to melt into his arms. Despite that one kiss, he'd not asked her out, or hugged her or kissed her again or anything. So why was he standing here, not moving? This non dating or dating thing, whatever it was they were doing, was hard.

Playfully, she reached out and touched his chest. "Excuse me, female coming through."

"Oh, I kind of like you backed into a corner," he teased as he stepped out of the way, and suddenly, she missed her wall.

"Trust me, you don't want to see me cornered," she said as she started walking toward the two doors on the side. One was the bathroom, and the other the bedroom, if she recalled. Smiling, she heard that low chuckle of his. It always delighted her.

"Oh, I've got the cure for spitting little kittens," he said. "Don't you worry about it."

"Oh, I wasn't," she said. "The bedroom is big enough, and the bathroom isn't nearly as bad as I remembered."

He looked into the bathroom. "Yeah, that wouldn't be too hard, I already know the plumbing and electric is good. Want me to work you up an estimate for renovating?"

"Yes, please," she said as they headed back down the stairs. "Then I'll decide if I'm doing it or not. Think of the commute to work! Just roll out of bed and there I am!"

"Would you go fishing with me tomorrow?" he asked her.

"Fishing?" She looked over at him.

"Yeah, you know. Little boat ride, some fishing, a picnic on the beach," he said. "We could make a day of it or I could have you back here early afternoon. Either way."

When was the last time she'd had an actual day off? Or fishing? Or a boat ride? Or a– "Yes, I'd love to," she said.

"Good. We have a plan."

She loved a plan.

Chapter 4

"**A**re you serious?" she asked him. What was the man thinking?

"I am," he said. "I thought taking you out for a day to relax would help you unwind, but it didn't. You are still wound tighter than fishing line."

"I am not," Jordyn said. Well, sure she was preoccupied. Who wouldn't be? She had a lot going on in her life! So many decisions to make and no one to make them with her. Everything, good, bad or ugly, was hers and hers alone. Sink or swim. Yes, her stress level was a little high and no, a day of doing nothing had actually exacerbated it, instead of calming her down. No one's fault. It had been her decision to go, but seriously? What did he want from her?

Then the home called and they had to cut their picnic short to run there to check on her mom who had fallen again and was all worked up. It had taken over an hour to calm her down. Plus she kept calling Ben Charlie – that was her uncle's name! And she called her mama. That was Grandma Rose.

After they left there, Ben drove to his house, despite her token protest. He'd just moved into his own house, out of

Miranda's where he'd been living since he moved to town. Ben had told her it wasn't his forever home, but a flipper house and she was interested in seeing it. The people on TV didn't live in their houses while they were flipping them, but he told her they didn't work another full-time job either and didn't actually do most of it themselves. He added they already had a house. He didn't and he was really tired of living with his sister. She could understand that.

Well, she thought it was a cute house anyway. It made her smile because it was decorated like hers. Sparsely. The only picture in the place was of a pretty blonde. She assumed it was Laura, but didn't want to ask.

There was a recliner chair, a TV, and probably a bed somewhere. Plus lots of tools. Lots of tools, just everywhere.

Remembering what he'd said earlier, though, she took a step backwards. "Ben, I've had a rough–" her voice trailed off. Rough what? Hour? Day? Week? Month? Year? "Besides. You can't!"

"Can't what?" he asked just as calmly as if he'd said something normal.

"You know!" Her anxiety ramped up. She did not need this right now. She needed to go home. Where was her purse? How far was she from the shop? That was where he'd picked her up and where her car was. If it was too far, she had half a dozen people she could call to come get her. Nice thing about living in Clearwater. Lots of friends around. Where were they when she needed them?

"Come here. A good cry is going to make you feel a lot better. I know things," he said.

Jordyn bit her lip and looked directly at him. "Ben!" Putting her hand over her pounding heart, she took a step back. "This isn't right," she said.

"I know women and I know you. You need a good cry and some good cuddling lap time," he said calmly, as if he weren't speaking some weird language she didn't understand. "You'll feel so much better after."

Jordyn shook her head. "That makes no sense, and besides, I don't think spanking is the way to do it. I know it isn't!"

"Then you'd be wrong," he said. "Now come on over here and park that pretty butt over my lap."

Why was she even tempted? She wasn't! Well, honestly, sitting on his lap and pouring out her woes to him seemed like it would be a great idea, but not that way!

"Maybe I should just sit on your lap and we can cuddle and talk?" she offered a sensible compromise, she thought.

"We could, but it wouldn't be what you needed," he told her. "Come on, you're making it worse by waiting."

"Am not," she countered. Brilliant. He'd spanked her once last week, for the first time, but that had been fun and playful, lighthearted and full of giggling which led to a lot of making out. She didn't think this one would be the same at all.

Her phone dinged and to stall, she pulled it out of her pocket and looked at it. "Great. Another delay on the sign. It won't get here in time! Why does everything go wrong at once?" Suddenly she did feel like crying, but that would only be tears of frustration, not of the pain he was planning to cause in her bottom.

Sighing, he stood up and grabbed her arm, walking her back to the chair, where he sat and pulled her over his lap. Why wasn't she fighting with him? What good would it do? She didn't even try to stop the choked sob that escaped her.

"Hope you are comfortable, 'cause you'll be here a while," he told her and brought down his hand on her bottom. What was she supposed to do? Just lay there and take it? No. She wasn't going to.

"Ben, stop it!" she complained.

"Sorry," he said. "No can do." And then he smacked her twice more. It didn't really hurt, but it wasn't pleasant.

"I'm serious," she said, but didn't make a move to get off his lap. She flinched, feeling the four quick smacks that came down again and was glad she was wearing her jeans. Why did she want him to take them down? She didn't. That would be ridiculous. She wanted them on. And wanted him to stop.

"Ben! No more!" she said, but that just made the smacks come harder and faster until she couldn't help squirming, trying to get away. "Okay! I'm done!" she said.

He stood her up, suddenly, and all she felt was disappointed and snappish. All she wanted to do was call him names like wimp and tell him to follow through on his promises.

"Drop the jeans, Jordyn," he said. "I'm tired of trying to get through to your brain with a denim barricade."

She shook her head, but her hand went to the button on her jeans. "No," she said, as she unzipped them. "No."

"Whatever," he said, and yanked them down. All she felt was a bit of relief, as strange as that sounded. He wasn't going to leave her high and dry, but would do the job well and properly. A tiny part of her felt grateful for that, but the smarter part of her brain was suddenly in flight mode and she took a step away, before he grabbed her and she was back over his lap with an *oof*.

"Be easy with me!" she begged. "Please!"

"Sorry, kiddo. I'm going to give you what you are needing and that's a good hard cry," he said, and brought his hand down on her panty clad bottom.

"Ow!" she cried out. That hurt a lot more than over her jeans! "Too hard!"

"Getting through," he suggested. "Let's get this going, shall we?"

"No!" she said and tried to wriggle away, but he held her

fast and close to him. It wasn't but a minute later she felt panic set in. How could she get away from this? "It hurts! No more!" His only response, it seemed, was to spank harder and faster. How could she make this stop? "Okay! No more, no more!"

He didn't even bother to answer her, but just steadily kept up a rhythm of pain on her already sore bottom. He might be silent, but she couldn't stop.

"No! I can't, please, please!" Her legs began to kick and her hand flew back to try and stop him. "No! I'll be good! It hurts, it hurts!"

The panic was deep seated now and she fought harder to get away, and that didn't seem to bother him at all. *"Ow!"* she screeched as he smacked her tender thighs four times and broke into sobs. That was just mean. He went back to her bottom but the dam had broken and she couldn't stop crying. Barely able to breathe, she gasped and sobbed and couldn't bring herself to fight anymore. It was no good, she couldn't. He was bigger and stronger and would spank her till he was done.

Then he was done.

There was something so satisfying about being held by a big guy, she thought as she put her head on his chest and sobbed. He just felt strong. This was her wall, the strength she'd been looking for, craving for so many years.

He patted her back and rubbed her shoulders while she cried. Why was she crying so much? She needed to stop but felt the stress attempting to leave her body. Should she let it? Why not? It would find its way back, she felt certain, but for now, it was lovely to just sit here and listen to his rumbly voice as he comforted her. She just hoped she stopped soon before she dehydrated.

As she finally calmed down, Jordyn realized he'd been right. She had needed a good cathartic crying session. Surely there were other, easier ways to do that, though, than going rear end up over his knees. There had to be. But for now, that didn't matter. She just felt better, and wanted to sit on his lap for... for what? Not forever. She didn't even know him that well, and besides, he wasn't really ready for a relationship yet. He'd implied as much and since she knew nothing about losing a spouse, she didn't know if or when he'd be ready. She needed to not rely on him, or count on him being hers.

However, for right now, his broad chest and strong arms were just what she felt like she needed. For this minute only, she reminded herself. Not for the long haul. Trying to get her sobs under control, she gave into her urge and cuddled as close as she could get to him.

Finally she sat up and he handed her a few tissues. Where had he gotten those? The mysteries of men. Blowing her nose, she snuggled back into his chest just for one more minute.

"You feeling better?" he asked her.

Jordyn nodded, wanting to lie, but why bother? It was true. "I do."

"Don't you have something to say to me?" He patted her back again.

"Like what?" she asked. She didn't want to talk about her problems right now.

"How about a thank you?" he asked.

"A thank you?" Jordyn felt dumbfounded. Why would she thank him for making her cry? "Why?"

"Because I gave you what you needed," he said.

"Yeah, don't hold your breath on that one," she said, feeling a little annoyed. "But, I admit, I do feel a little better. Nothing's really changed, I still have all the stress, but I just feel better, I guess."

"You are welcome," he said, entirely too smug for her taste, so she smacked his huge arm, then traced the part of his tattoo that stuck out with her finger.

"Doesn't mean I approved of your techniques," she

reminded him, but took a deep breath and noticed her chest didn't feel as tight anymore. Weird. Who ever said that a good cry didn't help anything? It must have, but now, she still had all the issues she had before. However, she did feel a little more confident she could handle them.

"One thing at a time," he told her as if he could read her mind. "This time next year, you will be busy in your fancy new kitchen and won't even remember these glitches that are making you so stressed out right now."

"Promise?" she asked as she put her head against his chest. Her wall. Her connection. The place where she felt grounded. Strange but true. Who would have ever thought she'd be attracted to a mountain man who liked to turn her over his knee? "And don't do that anymore."

"I promised the first one, but as to paddling your little butt, you seem to need that now and then." He pulled her closer to him, and she melted against him. If only she could stay here. What would it be like to wake up with him every day? Stiffening, she sat up. No. She couldn't think that. He wasn't ready. He might not ever be. How would she know? All she could do right now, though, was enjoy the moment. Soon she'd be too busy to worry about him, she hoped. Although she did give him the go ahead to remodel her apartment and had already notified her landlord she wouldn't be renewing her lease. So he'd be around. That almost tapped her out, though, or would when she paid for it all, so hopefully the bakery would open on time, and…

"Your mind racing again already?" he asked, and gave her a hug before standing her on her feet.

"Maybe," she confessed as he pulled her into one more hug.

"Next time I'll have to give you more, then." He laughed as she shook her head hard. "Okay, kiddo, almost time to get back to work. I'm glad I helped a little, though. Put your pants on."

"I'm glad too," she said, biting back the thank you words he'd demanded of her earlier. Nope. She was not thanking him for a spanking! Not going to and he couldn't make her. She reluctantly pulled her jeans up over her sore bottom.

"I do need to go to work," she said.

"Not till after we go eat," he said and grabbed her hand. "Confess, you are hungry, aren't you?"

"I don't have time," she said. Yeah, she was hungry. It was mid-afternoon and she'd been up since six this morning. She'd let her mom get in her head, and now needed to go to work, however, apparently, they were going to lunch. That was okay. She could handle a half an hour lunch.

Then she'd come back and do that supply order. A supply order! Her mouth curled in an almost smile before she realized he was looking at her. She certainly didn't want him thinking she was smiling about the spanking! No. Not at all. It was work and work only!

Later this evening, she was having dinner with Ellie and Lucy to discuss the Grand Opening in exactly one month. One month. Tomorrow was Ellie's second annual Wiener dog race. They were going to Ellie's and she'd be baking cupcakes in Ellie's kitchen. Mike was going out somewhere because as they all knew Lucy made him crazy. It was too bad she was married to his best friend.

Grabbing her purse, she followed Ben to the front door as he opened it for her. "Are we walking to the diner?" she asked him.

"Nope, we're walking to the truck, and I'm taking you out to the Garlic Knot for Italian," he said.

"We are? We have time for that?" she asked him.

"We have time for that," he said. "We need a break and I promised you a nice lunch, which got interrupted. We also might need a glass of wine which we can't get at the diner." He opened the truck door for her and smacked her butt as she climbed in.

"Hey!" she said. "That's still sore!"

"That's for not telling me thank you," he said.

"You haven't fed me yet," she said, being deliberately obtuse.

"Hangry women and I don't get along," he told her. "You'll feel better after you eat while sitting on your sore bottom."

"Ha ha," she said. However a big plate of pasta and some of their famous garlic knots and a glass of wine did sound really good. Plus she had good company if she could relax enough to enjoy it, and for some reason she thought she could. It had nothing to do with her spanking, though.

The Garlic Knot was at the edge of town, and as they pulled up, she saw Mike and Ellie walk out and waved. Suddenly, Jordyn hoped her eyes weren't red from crying. No one could see her spanking red bottom, thank goodness.

"Hey, you all!" Ellie bounced over to them. "Late lunch? How's the bakery coming, no, don't tell me now, wait till tonight when I have time to hear all the details. Right now, I have to run to the fairgrounds to make sure things are coming along for tomorrow. Ben, you are coming early in the morning, right?"

"Yes, ma'am," he said. "I'll be there with my toolbelt."

"Good, I'm so excited! Jordyn, the shrimp alfredo was excellent today! Will see you all soon!" She waved as she all but danced to their car.

Mike shook his head and said, "She wears me out," as he followed her to the car.

"They make an odd couple," he told Jordyn as he opened the door for her.

"They do, don't they?" she agreed. "But they seem happy, so that's what is important."

"You're right. Two today, please," he told the hostess.

Jordyn looked around as they followed the hostess to the table. Oh, no, there was Miranda. That was all she needed today. However, she noticed Miranda just got up and walked out the door. She had to have seen them. Ben was hard to miss. Maybe she had an appointment. That was probably what it was. At least she didn't have to deal with Miranda's oh so subtle put downs and condescension today. She smiled as she and Ben slid into a booth. "This is very nice," she said. "Thank you for the invitation."

"How's the butt?" he asked.

"We are not discussing such things in a public place!" she said primly, opening her menu. "It isn't very gentlemanly of you to ask."

"But how will I know if I don't ask?"

"Hush and buy me wine," she said.

"I always do what's needed," he reminded her and she couldn't help but smile back at him.

Yeah. He did.

"So. You and Ben?" Lucy asked her while she nibbled on a cookie.

Jordyn shook her head as she slid the first batch of cupcakes into the oven. "I don't think so," she said. "He lost his wife a few years ago and I think he's just looking for a friend. Pretty sure he's not ready for a relationship."

"Oh, I didn't know." Ellie looked stricken. "That has to be so hard for him."

"I don't think I knew anyone who lost a spouse at our age,

unless it was a divorce," Lucy said. "And you know in my circles, that isn't common either."

Lucy came from a very strict background. People married young and for life, and she and her sister Moriah had both fled when they were set up to be married at seventeen. "What happened?"

"Fast acting cancer," Jordyn said, hoping she wasn't over-stepping her bounds.

"I thought they got divorced," Mike said, walking in while zipping his jacket. "I didn't know Laura died."

"Did you know her?" Ellie asked him. Her husband nodded.

"I did. We all hung together in college. She was a livewire. Ben fell for her hard. I heard they got married but we'd grown apart by then. I feel bad for him." He walked over and kissed the top of Ellie's head. Not hard to do, he was six three to her five almost three. "I can't imagine losing you."

"You are stuck with me," she said. "I'm sorry about your friend."

"Thanks," he said. "I'm heading out. You girls have a good night and try to behave, or you know what will happen." He smiled as she laughed. "I mean it."

"Go away," she said. "Have fun with your buddies. We have girl things to talk about."

"Bye, Mike," Lucy said sweetly. "We will miss you!"

Jordyn laughed. That had to rankle him. He just waved and walked out. "What did you ever do to him?" she asked Lucy as she started mixing another batch of cupcake batter. This one was strawberry lemonade, the other had been vanilla pumpkin. People loved pumpkin anything, especially as fall arrived.

"Oh, Max says I'm just me," Lucy giggled as she grabbed another cupcake. "I don't take it personally. I think most of it is an act anyway."

"We all have our relationships," Jordyn said.

"So back to yours and Ben's," Ellie said. "He's a hunk. He's even bigger than Mike!"

"Big isn't everything," Lucy said primly. "But I mean, he's big!"

"He is," Jordyn agreed. "And he's funny and smart, and a hard worker and listens to me, and well…"

"Well?" Ellie pressed.

Jordyn shrugged as she poured batter into the cup molds. "I don't think he's ready for another relationship. He said he hadn't dated since Laura died. I don't want to be a rebound or a replacement or something."

"Then why are you hanging out with him?" Lucy asked. "You are just going to get your heart broken, because, girl, it sounds like you are falling for him."

Jordyn sighed. "I don't know. That's a good question. I do like him. But, well, guys, really – Miranda is his sister."

Ellie giggled and Lucy smiled. "Yeah, that is a problem," Ellie said.

A big one," Lucy agreed. "Is she helping you design your apartment?"

Jordyn shook her head. "No, she did a great job on my store, but I really don't need her in my personal space. Besides," she swept her arm around, "I don't have a grand and glorious mansion like some people. Just a little three-room apartment. Ben and I can figure it out just fine."

"Ben and I?" Ellie frowned. "Lucy is right. You are getting too attached."

Jordyn shrugged. "I don't know what to do. It's another couple of weeks before he's done with the shop, and then he said my apartment will take through the holidays."

"When is your lease up?" Lucy asked.

"End of December," she said. "No matter how it looks, or

how close it is to being done, I'll be living there come January first."

"You can always stay with me," Lucy said. "Or Mike and me," Ellie agreed. "You have options, Jordyn."

"Thank you both," Jordyn said as she pulled one batch of fragrant cupcakes out of the oven and put another one in. "Is Moriah doing well at her new job?"

Lucy nodded. "Little sister is doing fine. Seems to be enjoying life."

"That means she's running wild and Lucy doesn't approve," Ellie said.

"She's not running wild!" Lucy protested. "She's just, well, she's…"

"Acting like a normal eighteen-year-old?" Ellie said. "Working and going to school and hanging out with friends."

"I just worry," Lucy said. "She's so young."

"How old were you when you broke free and basically came to live with me and my grandma?" Ellie said. "Sixteen, seventeen?"

"The difference is, I had you and your grandma. Moriah has, well, I'm not sure who she has."

"She's living with and nannying for Heidi and her husband and their forty hundred kids," Jordyn said. "I talked to her just last week to see if she could help me out over the holidays because I'm hoping to be crazy busy. She's going to work for me part time when school is out. Heidi okayed her being gone in the mornings. She has some skill in the kitchen, you know. Learns quickly and takes direction well. Plus she's fun to be around. Not as fun as you, of course…" She smiled at Lucy. "But still fun!"

"That's okay." Lucy laughed as she leaned over to smell a cupcake. "I already have a full-time job, and I'm not Ellie. I can't do fifty things at once and besides, the mean ol' boss man wants me home when he gets there."

Ellie looked a bit uncomfortable and Jordyn figured it could be because her mean ol' husband wanted her home a little bit more than she was, too. She knew they'd had a problem when Mike demanded she close her real estate office when she got the city manager job. Ellie had wanted to keep it open and work part-time there, but he'd said either that job or the committees, but she wasn't doing all it. She'd reluctantly closed the office. Compromise was a price you had to pay to have a handsome hunk of a husband, apparently.

"Speaking of jobs," Ellie said. "Let's talk about your grand opening. It's time to get it set up! You still on course for November first?"

Nodding as she got out her icing supplies, Jordan said, "I am! Except for the sign. It's been held up for some reason."

"Well, worst thing that can happen is we order a quickie banner to go where the sign is," Lucy said. "We can put that up, and then when the sign gets there, maybe do a little social media blitz of it going up. That way you will have another little burst of free publicity."

"I'll go ahead and order the banner tomorrow," Jordyn said. "I really want the sign. Beth did such a great job designing it, but that's a good idea."

They went over a few more plans and the timeline. "I can't believe I will be open soon," Jordyn said. "It's just a dream come true."

"You've worked really hard for it," Ellie said. "I'm so pleased there will be another thriving business downtown and looking forward to seeing your place all done. It will look gorgeous, I'm sure."

"Of course it will," Lucy agreed. "After all, Miranda designed it!"

"Is she doing something with the Garlic Knot that you know about?" Jordyn asked. "Remember when Ben and I ran into you and Mike out there the other day? Miranda was there too, and seemed to be alone. Not that there is anything wrong with eating alone, I was just being nosy I guess."

"Who knows?" Ellie said. "She seems to have her finger in a lot of cupcakes around town. I know Mike and I run into her fairly often while we are out, though I don't think I saw her that day." She frowned as she moved a platter of finished cupcakes into the prepared box. "Do you have enough boxes made up or do I need to fold some more?"

"I think I made enough," Jordyn said. "Anyway, I ordered the shirts and they should be here in the next few days. I have the supply order in and my pantry is starting to look like a pantry instead of a catch all."

"I have the media on alert and what passes for some social media influencers in our little town on alert. I promised them samples," she told Ellie. "But I cleared that through Jordyn first, of course."

"Well, baking is my life!" Jordyn waved her frosting bag dramatically.

"Thank goodness, because you'll be doing it from here on out," Ellie said. "And not just for free!"

"We all give in our own way," Jordyn said. "I'll just be glad to have my own kitchen to do things in, and not working in someone else's all the time."

"It is going to be so fun for you! I am so looking forward to this next part of your life. New store, new apartment, new life, maybe a new boyfriend!"

Jordyn laughed and shook her head. If they only knew what the mountain man did to her – both emotionally and physically. Some things though, you didn't even tell your best friends. What would they think if they knew he gave her serious butterflies and then, also, spanked her? They'd be appalled, she felt sure. It sure wasn't anything she was going to tell them!

She yanked her head up shocked, biting back a gasp when

Lucy said, "I need to get home before curfew or my husband will blister my rear and I don't need that!"

"Lucy!" she gasped out before she saw Lucy's silly grin. "Oh, you're teasing." Surely no one else got spanked but her!

"Of course I am." Lucy flipped back her now golden blonde hair. "But just in case I'm not, I have to get going. Jordyn, I'll be in touch in the next few days about the details when I get them set up. Ellie, Juliet, Gypsy and I will see you tomorrow at the Weiner dog races!"

"Unless you are grounded," Ellie teased and Lucy made a mad, overly dramatic dash to the door, while Ellie and Jordyn giggled. "She never changes, does she?"

"Thank goodness," Jordyn said. "It's nice to have stability in your life. Where you know what you are getting. There. All done. Want me to help carry them to the car?"

"No, that's fine, Mike is helping me in the morning. Thanks for doing this, Jordyn. I really appreciate it."

"I am glad to help," she said. "And it's good practice for when the shop opens. Weirdly, this is the first time in years I haven't been either cooking or baking for someone every day."

"That has to feel strange, but it won't be long now!" Ellie said as they finished cleaning and Jordyn packed her supplies.

"It won't," she said as Mike came in.

"All done, Jordyn? Here, let me help you carry your stuff to the car."

Driving home, Jordyn felt a small pang of something. What? Envy of Lucy and Ellie having someone to come home to? Maybe a little bit. If that was what she wanted, and she didn't know if it was, could she ever have that with Ben? And if she wanted it with Ben, was he wanting the same thing? Was he ready for it? If not, could she wait till he was? What if he never could be? If he'd had the love of his life and then that was it? She was just a space filler or something, maybe?

Sighing, she unlocked the door to her stark apartment and

vowed, at least, to make her new one a little more homey, more welcoming and inviting. Some place she wanted to be, instead of being just a space filler. There was probably enough of that in her life already.

Jordyn looked up from her computer as Ben walked in the door the next day. "Morning," she said. "Look! My coffee maker came in!"

"Is hooking it up on my honey-do list?" She laughed and shook her head. He said, "Looks pretty fancy."

Jordyn laughed. "No, I already hooked it up. Want a cup?"

He shook his head. "Thanks, but I already had my fix today. However, the lemonade shake up machine is set up over at the fairgrounds. Want to go show me what a Weiner dog race is all about?"

Jordyn started to shake her head, she had so much work to do, and had planned to spend the day catching up on paperwork and seeing what all was in all the boxes that had arrived the last few days. Sure, she ordered them, but still, everything that arrived made her shop seem a little cozier and a little more real. However, a couple of hours wasn't going to hurt. Things would still get done.

"Sure!" she said. "When do you want to go?"

"I need to work on the exhaust fan, so half an hour."

She nodded, and ignored the little thrill that went through her. She got to spend some time with Ben. Time not working around here, not that there was anything wrong with the time they spent together here. However, usually there were other people around, running in and out, and they were all focused on getting something done. When they left here, she could focus on him and she liked that. What was it about this mountain man that she found so, well, butterfly worthy? Why was he so attractive to her? She'd met many men, but there was something about Ben that made her lose focus on anything but him. She didn't know if she liked that feeling, loved it, or hated it. Losing focus on her business was the dumbest thing she could do right now. The smartest thing she could do would be cancel her apartment remodel and send him on his way in two weeks when he was done with the store.

Was she planning to do that? Sadly, no.

It might not last but surely she could enjoy it while it did, right? It might be stupid, but if it was, she was going to embrace the stupid. Even if it smacked her in the butt now and then.

"You ready?" He emerged from her kitchen and asked a while later. "Got your exhaust fan working now. The reason it wasn't was a faulty switch."

Jordyn frowned. "It shouldn't come with a faulty switch."

"It doesn't have one now," he told her. "No problem."

"Does that void my warranty or anything?" she asked.

"I'm your warranty," he said, and unhooked his tool belt while she watched. That was a flat-out sexy act.

"Okay, if you say so," she said, closing her laptop.

"Have I lied to you yet?"

"If you have, I haven't caught it." She stood up and stretched, watching him watch her. "I'm ready. Have you really never seen a Weiner dog race?"

"Only on TV," he said. "Who knew there were that many around here? Enough for a race?"

"Dachshunds are a very popular breed," she informed him. "People love them."

"And love to watch them run apparently," he said as he opened the door for her. "Don't forget to lock up."

Jordyn rolled her eyes at him. "Yes, Daddy."

"Just reminding you to be safe," he said as they walked to his truck.

"Why would you think I wouldn't be safe? This is Clearwater. Nothing ever happens here."

"Then why do you have a police force?" he asked as he opened the truck door.

"Because that is what towns do," she said as she climbed in, waiting for the inevitable butt smack he always gave her as she got in. He didn't disappoint. He enjoyed smacking her butt, didn't he? She wondered what the attraction was, but decided not to ask. She probably didn't want to know and didn't want to earn a trip over his lap anyway.

"Well, of course, that makes sense," he said.

"So, what else are you working on besides my place?" she asked him as they drove across town to the fairgrounds. "Are you keeping busy?"

"Well, my next big project is this sweet little apartment over a cute little bakery," he said, smiling at her. "But other than that, Miranda has several businesses we are putting bids on, and hope to get."

"Is the Garlic Knot one of them?" she asked, remembering seeing her there.

He shook his head. "No, why? You hear something about a remodel there?"

"No," she said. "Just was curious. Look, I think the event is twice as big as it was last year." She looked at all the booths, and tents, the food trucks and cars lined up in the parking lot. "Ellie knows how to throw a party, doesn't she?"

"Mike has his hands full keeping that one under control," Ben said.

Jordyn looked at him. "Under control? What does that even mean?"

Ben chuckled, and as always, that low sound made her shiver. There was just something about him and his laugh that made her, well, all want-y and melt-y. It was silly, but true. "Ellie has too much on her plate, all the time. She seems to do it all with ease, but what's the driving force behind her always having to go and plan and do and be out and about?"

"Politics," Jordyn said. "Ellie has big political plans. She was a realtor for a few years while she did the events to get her name known, then this city manager job sort of fell in her lap. She now has her sights set on mayor next, then who knows."

"Never thought Mike would end up with a girl like her." Ben parked the truck in the lot. "I figured he'd find a little mousy stay-at-home housewife who'd pop out a dozen kids in a dozen years."

"What century do you live in?" Jordyn said, knowing by now to wait till he came to open her door. "There aren't women like that anymore. We all have to work for a living. A friend of mine, Heidi, has at least half a dozen kids and she still works as a nurse. Very few people have the luxury of staying home. Besides, I personally think it isn't very smart to totally rely on a man for all your financial needs. What if he leaves you and you are stuck with a fifteen-year gap in your resume and no recent skills? Not smart."

"What if he doesn't leave you and you have fifteen years of a happy home life and well-adjusted kids?" he asked, as if he really meant it.

"How do you know that will happen?" Jordyn shook her head. "It is just too iffy. Too scary. You need, at least, to keep your skills up to date, just in case."

"Living life just in case something bad happens doesn't sound very trusting to me," Ben said.

"Obviously, you don't read as many advice columns or talk to as many women as I do," Jordyn said. "You'd be surprised how many miserable women there are who feel trapped because he makes the money. Lucy would be a good one to talk to about it. She came from the background of marry young, stay home and have the babies. No other options.

Many of those women are just doubling down in order to convince themselves they are happy."

Ben shook his head. "I'll have to do that sometime. But right now, we're getting us a lemonade shake up and looking at all the animals." He paid their admission and they went inside the gate.

She looked around, marveling at how many more vendors and trucks were here than last year. Imagine it in five years, she thought. Ellie just had a knack for organizing and promoting this kind of thing. All Jordyn did was bake cakes, cookies and cupcakes. Maybe her mom was right. "No!" she said unexpectedly out loud.

"No, what?" Ben asked her and grabbed her hand.

"Sorry." She smiled and shook her head, flipping her braid back over her shoulder. "My mom's voice jumped in my head suddenly. Probably because we were talking about jobs. She thinks I should be a nurse."

"If you were a nurse, who'd bake the cupcakes?" he asked, leading them down a side path.

"Anyone can bake cupcakes, according to my mother," Jordyn informed him.

"Not as good as you do it," he said.

"That's a sweet thing to say," she told him.

"I'm just a sweet person," he said. "Unless you need a good paddling. Then I'm an ol' meany."

Jordyn giggled, but decided to drop that subject. "Look! There's the lemonade stand. Do you think if I made those at the bakery they'd be as good as here?"

"I'm sure they'd be great," he said, ordering two large ones. "But I think a lot of these are the atmosphere."

She had to agree with that. There was just something about wandering around the fairgrounds, the smell, the people, the warmth of the sun, watching the person shake it like a bartender that made a lemonade taste extra good.

"There's Ellie!" She pointed out a crowd of people surrounding her small friend, as she stood in the middle with a clipboard in hand. "Let's steer clear or she will put us to work."

"Good idea," he said, and led them down a different path where there were jewelry and craft booths and sign makers, people were so crafty.

"Oh, look, there's the puppies," she said. The animal shelter that this event was held for always brought out adoptable dogs for the crowd to see and pet.

"Do you want a puppy?" he asked as they reached over the fence to pet the jumpers.

Jordyn shook her head. "No, I work too much. It isn't fair to the dog to be home alone all day, especially when I'm getting started. If I need a doggie fix, I go visit Lucy and Max, they have two dogs."

"How about a cat?" he said, picking up an adorable little terrier of some kind, after putting his drink on the ground.

"Cat hair in a bakery? I think not!" she said. "I'm just fine starting up my new business without having something else to take care of. Maybe one day. How about you? Dog or cat person?"

"Me? I like to fish," he said, "but I don't think that counts as making me an animal lover."

Jordyn giggled as they both cleaned their hands with the offered wipes and picked their drinks back up. "No, I really don't think it is."

"Hey, Jordyn. Hi, Ben." Joni stopped them as she wandered around. "Have you seen Ellie?"

"Yes, she's over there." Jordyn motioned the way they'd come. "Well, she was ten minutes ago at least. What did she rope you into doing?"

"I'm supposed to judge the Weiner dog race," Joni sighed. "But so is her brother and I'm not speaking to him right now."

"Well, don't volunteer me in your place," Jordyn said. "Ben and I both have to get back to work soon."

"Oh, I'll probably do it," Joni said. "I mean, he lives next door and we work in the same building. I can't avoid him forever."

"No, I know you can't." Jordyn smiled. "Good luck!"

Ben grabbed her free hand again as they walked and she felt that shiver again. She liked that shiver. "They do that a lot, don't they?" he said.

"What, make up and break up? Yeah, but it seems to work for them, I guess," she said.

"I don't work like that," he said. "Too much drama for me."

"Some people apparently thrive on drama," she told him. "Look, there's the pet parade! Let's watch! I bet Lucy is in it."

An hour later, they headed back to the truck. "So what was your favorite?" she asked him. "The parade or the race?"

"People sure are wild about their animals, aren't they?" he countered. "I don't think I've ever seen so many dogs in one place."

"It makes a lot of money for the shelter, and gets them publicity so people know more of what they do and offer," Jordyn said, climbing in the truck.

"And gets Miss Ellie's name out there," he noted.

"Well, now, that's just a little extra perk for her hard work, isn't it?" Jordyn smiled. "I feel like I need a shower and clean clothes before I go back to work. So much dog hair! Can you drop me off at my car?"

"Whatever you prefer, ma'am," he said, driving to where her car was parked behind the bakery. He leaned over and kissed her lightly on the forehead. "Thanks for a fun afternoon. I'll see you soon."

"Thank you," she said, and reached for the truck door, but he leaned over further and opened it from the inside.

"There you go," he said.

Jordyn climbed out of the truck, feeling a little let down. What was with that? He too lazy to get out and walk around the truck? He was the one who trained her not to get out before he opened the door. See you soon? What did that even mean?

Watching him drive away, Jordyn shook her head. She was being ridiculous. He was going to a job, she felt certain. He'd see her soon because he'd see her soon. The forehead kiss was sweet. Things were fine. So why did she feel so weird?

Chapter 5

"You are in a mood today," Lucy said, as she packed her case up to leave. "I hope you get to feeling better."

"I'm sorry, Luce. It isn't you," Jordyn said.

"Hey, I watch reality TV! I know how high-strung chefs are! I've seen them beat up pans, and walk off jobs, and throw tantrums and cuss people out, and…"

Jordyn smiled and held her hand up. "Point taken! I'm not that bad! But we all have our moments. Even you, I'm sure."

Lucy shook her pink hair and said, "Nope. Not me! I always walk the straight and narrow. Will get back to you with the final details on the grand opening celebration details as soon as I get them tied up. Go eat something. You know how you get when you are hangry and you are right there." She all but skipped out the door.

How Lucy managed to always be in a good mood was beyond her. Her upbringing, where women had to 'keep sweet' all the time and weren't allowed to show other emotions? Jordyn hoped Max encouraged her to throw a tantrum now and then or be anything but sweet.

She hadn't heard from Ben in three days and she was beyond pissed. It was less than two weeks before she wanted to do her soft opening, which was not set in stone, but he knew it. She still had things to do around here. Though she half smiled as she looked around, it was looking very good. The little tasting room was even cuter than she'd thought. Miranda had hired a local artist to come in and paint a mural on her picture wall. It had been a picture of Lake Clearwater's scenery. The lake was crystal clear, sparkling blue with a few swans floating around. There were towering pine trees and a red picnic table just waiting for someone to come along and fill it with wonderful food and laughter. You could almost smell the air and the trees. The artist had done a wonderful job.

The gathering table was a gorgeous dark oak and seated twelve comfortably with room for two other small tables and a long bench under the window overlooking the park across the street. The curtains were simple linen and made the room feel warm and welcoming.

The kitchen was crisp and clean, all white and stainless steel and her pantry was beginning to feel stocked. Her utensils and new pans had come in just a couple of days ago and she'd loved washing and finding spots for them all. Both the bathrooms were functional and ready for use. The display and customer seating room was the last thing to be finished. Her cash register was to come in the next day or so, with someone coming to install it for her. How hard could it be? Wasn't it just like a computer you plugged in?

Reluctantly, she pulled one of the bistro chairs out of the box. Who knew they didn't come put together? Well, she should have, she guessed. And what did she have? A dozen of them? While she could do it, putting stuff together wasn't her favorite thing to do. Maybe she'd hide in her office and hope a magic fairy came and put them together for her? Or like she learned in Girl Scouts, a magic Brownie.

She smiled, thinking of the picture of her and Ellie in their little brown beanie hats. Lucy hadn't been allowed to join. Sighing, she went to the kitchen, – her kitchen! – to get some tools. Going back, she found her phone and turned on her favorite radio channel. She didn't have any idea what was going on in the world, so a little news and some classic rock would help soothe her nerves, she hoped.

Three chairs in, she decided she didn't care if Ben showed up or not. Probably better that he didn't, or she'd give him a piece of her mind and then she'd end up over his knee. Yeah. Probably not a good idea. How dare he think he could spank her anyway? What kind of man did that? Why had she not only allowed it, but was compliant about it? It was ridiculous. What had she been thinking? Well, it was certainly nothing that would ever happen again, she knew. As a strong, proud, independent, soon to be successful woman, there was zero reason she should allow herself to be spanked. She didn't like it. It was embarrassing, humiliating, painful and even the fact she adored curling up on his lap after didn't make up for that. Now that one time had been fun. She almost smiled as she put the finishing touches on the third chair and set it aside to grab the fourth box.

What had they been arguing about? Oh, that's right, if the books were better than the movies. She much preferred curling up on the couch or munching popcorn in a theater with a movie. He said there were very few movies that could hold a candle to the book. She asked him how many books and movies he had read and seen to compare and they were off. Before she knew it, they were bantering and laughing and somehow she found herself across his lap. How had he done that?

He'd smacked her bottom and said, "Now who is right?"

"Brute force doesn't make you right," she'd said and giggled, "it just makes you bigger and stronger."

"And smarter." He'd smacked her again and she realized for sure that he was only playing. Well, two could play.

"Nah, only mountain men manhandle their women," she'd told him and wiggled her bottom at him. That would teach him.

"Manhandle? You think this is manhandling, do you?" He'd smacked her bottom a few more times, while she obligingly yipped.

"Hey, it isn't my fault you can't see the nuances in a movie and have to have the printed word!" Her bottom had begun to feel nice and warm.

"Nuances? I'll give you nuances." He peppered her bottom with a series of light smacks while she giggled and wiggled. This kind of spanking she could get behind.

"Is that all the nuance you got?"

He obligingly picked up the nuances a few degrees. "Ouch!"

"Oh, I'm sorry," he'd said. "Was that not nuanced enough for you?" He smacked her well warmed bottom a little harder then and instead of feeling pain, she'd felt something else. Turned on? Maybe.

Jordyn shook her head. Spankings shouldn't turn her on. Though she had done a little research and it seemed it really wasn't that big of a secret that many women were turned on by them – and some men too. Not only giving but receiving. She smiled as she tightened a screw thinking of spanking Ben. Yeah. That wasn't happening. Why wasn't what was good for the goose, good for the gander? Why did she care when she'd just decided not to allow him to spank her again?

"It didn't matter," she said out loud. Of course it didn't. She needed to put all things spanking and kissing and more and Ben out of her mind. She had a shop to open and chairs to put together. There was a long list of need to do's on her computer, also. Her soft opening was coming up and

November first was right around the corner. Apparently Mayor Lydia would be at her ribbon cutting ceremony! That was a pretty big deal, even if her best friends had direct access to her. The paper would be there, and the radio station. They weren't big enough for a TV station but Lucy was trying to get one from St. Louis to come down, just for a slice of Americana piece. No luck so far, but who knew what they might come up with. She needed to remember to wear makeup opening day, she decided. She had been slacking on it while working in the dusty construction site that was her shop.

Now, though, her shop was starting to look like a real bakery. Not perfectly clean yet, but getting there. The health department was due in early next week, and she hoped to get an all clear. At the very least she'd have a little time to fix anything, though while it was a concern, she wasn't really worried. She knew what she was doing in the kitchen.

With men, however, that was an entirely different story. She knew nothing about them. That guy in college. Well, she thought he had been an exciting dominant personality, but instead he'd been a controlling bully. She didn't want that again, even though she craved Ben's power and control. Was she making the same mistake again? Was she simply doomed to be drawn to the wrong kind of man? And did it matter? He hadn't been in touch with her for three days now, after all.

Ben looked over at his annoying little sister. "I don't know what you are talking about," he said, as calmly as he could while picking up his fork. Why wasn't he here with the gorgeous little baker with the sweet little giggle and the long brown braid that she kept flipping over her shoulder? Instead he was having lunch with Miranda. Why? She'd asked him, of course. "I thought this was a working lunch."

"Of course it is," she said, in her perfectly articulated way that drove most people crazy. It made her sound snooty. The fact she was snooty had nothing to do with it. "However, I'm allowed to worry about my baby brother."

"I'm your big brother and I'll warm your butt to remind you if you need me to," he said.

"Oh, hush. You haven't done that since we were both children." She sliced her fish then squeezed some lemon on top.

"Doesn't mean I forgot how," he warned her.

"Yes. I'm frightened. There, are you happy?" She put her fish in her mouth and chewed, swallowed, dabbed her mouth with her napkin and said, "So, you and the baker?"

"So, you and a working lunch?" He didn't want to talk about this. About her. He didn't know what he was thinking, how could he explain it to her nosy self?

"Fine. We will get to work. I've got a couple of new businesses on the line but I need you to go out and do an inspection on one. I'm not sure they are worth our time. But now, I want to hear about you and the cookie maker." She put more fish in her mouth and stared at him.

"Her name is Jordyn and yes, I've seen her a few times," he said. "That's it. Nothing more."

"Umm-hmm. I'm sure," she said, looking at him with those piercing blue eyes that looked just like their mother's. "So?"

"Randy, I don't want to do this."

"Sometimes you have to do things you don't want to do for family," she said. "Like tell your sister how you are feeling."

"I'm fine," he said as she said it at the same time and then looked at him.

"I'm not satisfied with that answer."

"That's all you're getting."

"No, it isn't. You can say you have only seen her a few times, but I know better. I've seen you out and about in town and I've heard from people. Clearwater isn't that big. I also know she is your first serious one since Laura and I need to know, one, you are okay, and two, you aren't going to break her heart."

Well, that was different. "Why do you care about her heart?"

"I am trying to build a reputation in town and the last thing I need is the city manager's best friend thinking my brother, who is also my main contractor, is going around breaking hearts and being a cad."

"So it's all about you?"

His sister rolled her eyes. "Yes, the only thing I care about is me and my business. Quit acting like you don't know what I'm talking about."

He didn't say anything, but deliberately put a bite of his chopped steak in his mouth and stared at her. His little sister was afraid of nothing, he knew, and stared right back. "Ben? Talk to me. Are you ready for a relationship?"

"Randy, I don't want to discuss this with you. I appreciate your worry, I really do. I will do my darndest not to damage your reputation in town. And speaking of that, you might want to be a little more subtle following Mike Murphy around."

He waited and her reaction was just like he thought it would be. She paled and dropped her eyes. So he was right. She had moved here for Mike. Great. At least she hadn't done anything stupid yet. That he knew about.

He reached over and grabbed her hand. "We're a pair, aren't we? Let's blame it on the folks and call ourselves good, what do you say?"

"I don't know what you are talking about." She pulled her hand away from him and picked up her napkin again. "Now, let's talk about these jobs I'm considering."

Way to change the subject, little sis, he thought. Ben

decided since he didn't want to talk about Jordyn, it was just fine to have that working lunch he'd been promised.

He left the diner a while later and headed to his truck. He'd taken advantage of what was probably the last of the really nice weather here to go fishing the last few days. He was caught up on work, except for some finishing touches on the bakery, and then he'd start her apartment reno. Knowing women, she was probably upset he hadn't contacted her the last few days. Once you kissed a woman, they thought they owned you and you were required to phone or at least text them every day. He'd just needed to get away for a while. A couple of days out on the rented boat and then camping on the shore was exactly what he'd needed. Why live by such a gorgeous lake if you couldn't take advantage of it? He looked at a few houses, planning to buy one out there eventually. Maybe a fixer upper he could flip. Maybe not. He was in no hurry. He needed to flip the one he was in first, and then look around. Planning to be here for a while took the stress off flipping houses.

His feet found their way down the street to the bakery. He might as well go get it over with, see how mad she was. Did it matter? Yeah, actually it mattered a lot. He'd done a lot of thinking out there on the lake. He'd talked to Laura a bit and felt comforted that she'd want him to be happy, but he promised not to use her favorite flogger on anyone else ever. A sense of comfort and peace had come over him out there and he felt as if he were ready to move on. The little baker was as far from Laura as a person could be. At least no one could say he had a type. And if it upset Mike and his wingman, then so much the better.

The lights were on in the bakery, so he knew she was there working. He'd go in and see what all she was doing and what kind of trouble he was in.

The door was locked, so he took out his key ring and

unlocked it. He'd have to give her the key back after the apartment renovation, but until then, he had it.

Unlocking the door, he came in to see her sitting on the floor, surrounded by chairs and boxes.

"Hello, Jordyn," he said.

She looked up at him, and he could feel the tension coming off her in waves. That was okay, he was in that kind of mood, too. They could both use a good session. He locked the door behind him. Just in case.

"Hello, Ben," she said coolly. "You left some stuff in the kitchen."

"I know. I'll need them to finish up in there tomorrow." He looked at her sitting on the floor putting together chairs. She had about a half dozen of them done and looked to have half a dozen more. "Just came to put the bench together for the tasting room this afternoon."

"Okay," she said, but didn't look at him. Yup, she was mad, for sure. "It's in there."

"Think I'll bring it out here and work with you," he said, as if he didn't notice she was upset.

"Whatever," she said as she sat the next chair upright and then started putting the next one together.

Whatever. Oh yeah, those were fighting words all right. Well, he'd put the bench together first. Then maybe turn her cute little butt over it, and paddle it thoroughly for her. It was obviously what she was asking for, and he was the man for the job. Well, she wasn't controlled enough for that yet. She'd wiggle right off. Over his knee she'd go, and that was just fine too.

He smiled as he pulled the bench parts out into the display room. Teaching her a little lesson was just exactly what he needed to polish off his few days being off properly.

She sat silently putting together the chairs and he smiled, knowing she was ready to explode at any minute. Yeah, he should have at least told her he was going fishing for a few days. Why hadn't he? He had just felt the need to get away and actually had left at three in the morning. Didn't mean he couldn't have left her a message or texted her when he got there or something, but instead, he'd just shut his phone off. It had actually been wonderful for him. For her, obviously, not so much. Nothing he could do about it now, but make it up to her the best way he knew how.

"So did you have a good couple of days?" he said, laying out the parts for the bench on the floor.

"Yes." Her voice sounded icy.

"Good. I did too. Went to the lake, went fishing for a few days. I'll have you over for some fish on the grill soon. Caught a big wall eye, bunch of blue gill."

"That's nice," she said, as she set up another chair and gave it a shake, presumably to test it out.

"Yeah, I needed to get away for a few days. Anything come up while I was gone?"

"No. You aren't indispensable," she said, and pulled another chair out of the box.

"Never said I was," he said. He got up and went to the kitchen to turn on the audio system he'd set up last week. This place needed some noise before her voice iced him out. While he was there, he grinned and saw the utensils set up in their containers on the shelf, and grabbed a thick wooden spoon. You never know when one might come in handy. There, some nice classic jazz and an implement for later.

He settled back down in front of the bench and finished building it in what he hoped was companionable silence, but really, he knew better. It didn't take him long to finish it, then he stood up and said, "Hey, Jordyn, can you grab the other end of this so we can get it set up in the little room?"

Not saying a word, she got up, putting down her Allen

wrench on top of the chair seat, and grabbed the end of the bench.

"Ready?" he asked her and she didn't answer, but shrugged. So he picked up the other end and headed toward the wide door opening. It didn't take long for them to get it settled in place and he stepped back and looked around. "Looking good in here, Jordyn. What more needs done?"

"Curtain rods," she said shortly as she went back to the other room.

He saw the rods in the corner, but decided to wait until after they had their upcoming discussion to hang them for her. That was more of a boyfriend job than a contractor job.

He walked back in the room and grabbed her arm. Then he reached down and took the Allen wrench from her hand. "Sit," he told her and marched her over to one of the completed chairs. Not to his surprise, she went along with him. She needed this 'talk' as much as he did. Women were so obvious.

He pulled her arm and plopped her into the chair where she sat, folded her arms and glared at him. He folded his and glared right back. "What?" she asked as if she had no idea.

"Yes. What?" He stood in front of her at his full height. She didn't seem a bit intimidated.

"I don't know what you are talking about," she lied right to his face as if she could get away with it.

"Want to try that again or get a paddling for lying?" He'd dropped his voice.

"You wouldn't dare." She didn't blink.

"Oh, don't you worry, you are getting that sweet little bottom warmed before long, but I'd be glad to do two for you, one for lying and one because you seem to be needing it," he said.

She narrowed her eyes and didn't say a word. "I mean it, Jordyn. Start talking."

"If I have to tell you," she started and he put his hand up.

"Don't even go there. Men are not mind readers and 'if I have to tell you' does not cut it. Use your words instead of your pouty face. That will work out better for you."

"You should know." Her voice was starting to rise a little.

"You tell me, and tell me now, and that's the last time I'm telling you," he warned.

He watched her take a deep breath and her shoulders shook. "You left."

There. Good start. "To go fishing," he agreed.

"And didn't call, but you didn't need to call and I don't know why I'm so upset but I am, so just leave me alone." That all came out in one big rush and he fought back a smile. Now they were getting somewhere.

"So you are mad because I didn't call or mad because you are upset I didn't call?"

"Yes," she said it almost triumphantly as if they'd accomplished a breakthrough.

"So, we are at a point in our relationship where I need to call you and let you know where I am," he said.

She looked confused, then blushed and looked down at her feet, and squirmed. "No. Maybe. I don't know."

"But when I didn't call you felt, how?"

"Hurt," she blurted out, then covered her face with her hands. "Unimportant," she whispered.

Okay. That one stung. "So I should have called and since I didn't you feel like you don't matter to me, am I right?"

"No!" she said defiantly. "No. I don't care. I just stupidly got my feelings hurt and it has nothing to do with you or anything to do with an us. This is about me and I'm fine."

She crossed her arms and stared determinedly at her shoes. "Jordyn, look at me," he told her.

"No," she said stubbornly. "I need to get back to work. I'm fine."

Rule number fifteen or something like that in the how to understand women handbook said quite clearly, 'I'm fine' does not mean they are fine at all. However, it was up to him to make sure she was fine. First he had to get her in the right frame of mind to accept his apology.

"Stand up and drop your pants." He picked up the wooden spoon he'd laid on the counter.

"I will do no such thing," she said and lifted her eyes to glare at him but her eyes homed in on the wooden spoon and she trembled just a little. "Put that back."

"I'm going to be introducing it to your pretty little bare bottom here in a minute," he told her and smacked his hand with it, and smiled when she flinched.

"You can't do that! It's unsanitary!"

"Unsanitary?" What did that even mean?

"Yes! You'll get butt oil or something all over it! I won't be able to use it in the shop!"

Butt oil? At least she'd accepted she was getting a spanking. "I guess I could take off my belt," he said. "Or I'll just buy you a new spoon and we can save this one for special."

"Ben," she started.

He waved the spoon at her and said, "Stand up and drop them. Now."

Reluctantly she stood up and her hand moved to her pants. "Ben," she started again.

"Now," he said. He always made sure he had consent before he did anything, and this was one way to gain it. She might not think she wanted a spanking but by dropping her pants, she was consenting to one. That was important to him. He and Laura had had a CNC – Consensual Non-Consent - relationship. She might not want what he was doing in the moment, but she'd given him blanket consent to do what he wanted whenever, barring her using her safeword. He needed to discuss that with Jordyn sometime, but not right now. Right now, he had a bottom to turn red.

"Don't look," she said.

Don't look at what? He didn't bother to answer that, but just waited. Finally, slowly, her jeans went down to mid-thigh. Her practical pink cotton briefs were left on but he decided they could and would come down later on. He'd also take her lingerie shopping later at some point.

"Ben? You don't have to do this," she managed to choke out. "Really!"

"Yet, I really think I need to," he said and stepped to the chair she'd vacated to drop her pants. He sat down and pulled her over his lap in one quick movement before she could think.

"Keep your hands on the floor," he said, and smacked her with the spoon.

"I won't!" she said, but put her hands down there. Well, he knew she wouldn't but he had to get her in the frame of mind to listen to him. And she was.

"Toes on the floor," he smacked her again and she whimpered as she did what she was told.

"Good girl, giving me a nice round bottom to paddle." He smacked her again.

Jordyn yipped, but said, "Yeah, that was my goal. To make things easy for you."

"Are you complaining?" He smacked her again and could see the spot start pinking up, so he focused on that area for a few more smacks just to watch it turn from pink to red until she wiggled the spot away from him.

"Stop wiggling," he told her.

"Stop spanking me," she said, but he noticed she still had her hands and toes on the floor. He wasn't making an impression yet, but she was trying.

He smacked that spot one more time and then gave her mercy and moved to cover her entire pink clad bottom. She wiggled and squealed adorably. There was just something about a woman over his knee that made him feel – well, he didn't know, dominant? He smiled thinking of how he – and Mike and Max – used to dominate. Now they had a power exchange and spanked their girls. Amazing how you mellowed in old age. He shook his head and focused on the bottom in front of him. She had her feet off the floor but wasn't kicking yet, and her hands weren't trying to protect her bottom, she could take a lot more.

"Stop it!" she demanded.

"Stop what? This?" He brought the wooden spoon down hard, right where she'd feel it when she sat, and then hooked a finger in her pretty pink panties. "Or baring your bottom?"

"Noo!" she wailed. "Stop!"

She wiggled and tried to twist away but he'd seen that move before, and managed to get them down to just below her thighs. Then he smacked her a few more times, holding her tightly while she began to react as if she felt it. "Ben, no more, no more!"

"We just got started good," he told her.

"I hate that spoon!" she wailed.

"This spoon?" he asked, and smacked her three or four more times, just to see if she could answer.

"No! Yes! I don't know! Okay! Done!"

"Not yet." Her bottom was turning a lovely shade of red and he had to catch her hand that was trying to cover her bottom. Her howls were sincere and he remembered she wasn't used to implements. He'd have to cut this short. He did, after all, want her over his knee many more times.

"Stop!" she screeched. "Please!"

"Had enough?" he asked her.

"Yes! Yes!" she sobbed out. "No more, please!"

"Are you going to be a good girl?" He smacked her with his hand after tossing the spoon to the floor.

"I'll be good!" she promised, sniffling loudly and taking very shaky breaths. "I will!"

He gave her three more just because he wanted to, then pulled her panties back up while she cried, and stood her up. She sank down to her knees in front of him and hugged his leg, wiping her tears on his pants. He let her calm down a minute, then when her sobs were under control put his hands under her arms and pulled her up on his lap. Her pants were still down around her ankles but he rather liked her long bare legs against him.

"You feel better now?" he asked as she cuddled against him as if she belonged there in his lap and in his arms.

Jordyn shook her head. "No. My bottom hurts and my nose is running."

"Normal consequences for just having gotten a well-deserved spanking," he said, trying not to smile.

"I wasn't that bad!" she said.

"But you feel better now, don't you?"

She shook her head against his shirt. "I don't and you owe me a new spoon."

"I'll make sure to get you one, but we'll hang this one on the wall for a future reminder for you to behave."

"Will not," she protested.

"I didn't do a very thorough job on that little bottom if you are still arguing with me," he teased. "You should be saying yes sir and no sir."

"Will do no such thing, Sir!" she said and sniffled once more. "I don't know why I got the spanking when you were the one who was bad."

"I was bad? Because I didn't call and tell you I was leaving."

"Yes."

"And?" he pressed her.

"And my feelings were hurt and I worried about you, and it was just mean," she said. "I have enough on my mind without having to worry about you and..." She stopped talking and buried her face in his shirt.

"And what, Jordyn?" he asked gently while he patted her back.

She just shook her head against his chest. "Nothing."

"Next time I'm going to paddle that stubborn out of you before I stop," he said.

"Will not," she mumbled. "I need to pull my pants up."

"No, you don't," he said, and held her tightly. "Not till we're done talking. I might need to give you a little more encouragement."

Once again, she shook her head. "No more! Please!"

"Not right now," he assured. "But you need to talk to me."

"You talk to me," she countered and leaned back to look at him.

Well, that was fair, he guessed. "I needed to think."

"And since you are male, you can't multitask. Think and make a phone call or text. I totally get it."

Ouch. "That's a fair assessment," he said. "I didn't call you because I didn't know what to say."

"The great Ben Collins at a loss for words? Hard to believe." She wiggled on his lap and tugged at her panties. He really wanted to pull them off her, but managed to refrain.

"I'm only a man," he said, and caught her hands in his. "I needed to think, so I went to think."

"And what did your thinking come up with?" she asked.

"That I'd probably need to paddle your butt when I got back because you'd be all pouty and mad." He kissed the top of her head.

"I guess you were right about that. Was that the only thing you thought about?"

"Person can do a lot of thinking out on the lake," he said. "You should try it sometime."

"I can think just fine while I'm kneading bread and baking cookies," she said. "I really want to pull my pants up now."

Reluctantly he let her stand up and chuckled as she turned around to pull them up and fasten them. Like sticking that nice red bottom in his face wasn't temptation at all. He noticed a little bruise developing right under the corner of her underwear. She'd appreciate that later. He didn't know why his women were so happy about their bruises because they sure squawked while they were getting them. Trying to leave them something to look at was a point of pride for him. They always mentioned it later.

"You feeling better?" he asked her after she turned around.

"I'm still a little ticked off," she said and rubbed her bottom. He almost told her to stop but she looked so adorable standing there with tears on her cheeks, sniffling, and rubbing her bottom, like the well punished little girl she was.

"I'm sorry for upsetting you," he said. "I will not leave without telling you again."

"Okay," she said reluctantly. "I still don't know what you were thinking about."

He shook his head. "You know men, we aren't deep thinkers."

"Liar," she said, and flipped her braid back over her shoulder. "But I guess I don't need to know right now."

"We will talk about it when the time is right," he said. "Right now, let's get the rest of these chairs put together before I have to leave. Hey, are you busy this afternoon?"

She looked around and said, "A little. Why?"

"I'm going out to the lake," he started but she interrupted. "Again? You just got back!"

"Not to think," he said and unloaded another chair to put

together. "I'm going out to do an estimate for a new BnB going up out there."

"Oh. Work. Well, thanks for telling me." She put her head down and kept working on the chair leg, but he noticed her fingers were trembling.

"Come here," he told her, stood up and opened his arms. He smiled when she didn't hesitate but rushed into them, dropping a screw that rolled across the floor. Pulling her into a hug, he asked, "Do you want to come with me? I'm just looking at some minor remodels for the new BnB going up out there."

Jordyn shook her head. "I'd really love to but the health inspector is coming early next week, and I really need to be ready. Plus I have to call a couple of people about their applications and set up appointments. I wish I could though. Thank you for asking me."

"Well, if the health inspector is coming you better do something with the spoon that has the butt oil all over it," he teased as he kissed the top of her head and let her go.

"Funny," she said, and he noticed as she picked the screw up off the floor, her hands were no longer shaking. Just needed a little reassurance, he figured. See, women just weren't that hard.

"I'll be here first thing in the morning," he told her. "Leave me a list of things that I can help you finish up. Are you doing a soft opening as soon as you pass the health inspection?"

Jordyn nodded, eyes sparkling. "Yes! I can't wait! Then there is the grand opening on November first. I remember when I first started this and thought it could be done in just a couple of weeks. I still haven't heard from my sign for out front, though." She went to a notebook on her little 'office' card table and made a note. "I'm going to miss working in this big room. I'll have all my office stuff set up back in the cubby office."

"You'll be out here plenty," he assured her. "Have you hired anyone yet?"

"I've scheduled interviews for new people at the end of the week. I want one at least permanently, and a couple of temporary for the opening and holiday rush. Lucy's sister Moriah is a good kitchen helper and is great with people, too. But she has another job so won't be here very much."

"This is going to be great," he said. "You'll be a big success."

"I hope so," she said. "I'll do the best I can."

"That's all you can do," he said. He finished the chair and reached for another. "Last one," Jordyn said as she finished hers and began to clean up the boxes. "It is really starting to come together. I just love it so much. As annoying as your sister is, she sure knows what she's doing."

"She does," Ben agreed. "And she really doesn't try to be annoying. She's just that way."

"Oh, I think she tries," Jordyn said. "She's way too good at it for it to be an accident."

"She'd be pleased to hear that," Ben said. He finished up his chair and stood up. "I guess I better go." Walking over to her, he stood in front of her and lifted her chin so she looked up into his eyes. "I'm sorry I didn't let you know I was leaving. I really don't ever want to do anything that hurts you."

"Except spank me?" She rubbed her bottom, but then sank into his arms as if she belonged there.

"Bottom-hurt clears the air. Mind-hurt muddies it up," he said as he kissed the top of her head.

"Says you," she mumbled, then said, "I accept your apology."

"Good girl," he said and hugged her till she squealed and giggled. "Okay. I really have to go. You sure you can't come?"

Jordyn shook her head. "I really can't. Hope you have good luck out there. So what is it again?"

"A new BnB," he said while picking up his tool belt. "Bryan's sister Jenna bought it. Remember, we met her at Mike's that night. I think Bryan and Alex are her silent partners. Anyway, Bryan's meeting out there, too."

"Oh, now I wish I could come. Tell them both good luck and I will see them soon."

"I'll call you soon," he promised her. "As soon as you have time, but before your soft opening, we will go out to dinner."

"Sounds great," she said.

He walked over and kissed her once more, then walked out the door before he swept her off her feet and ravished her. She had to work and so did he.

Ben walked down the street toward his truck. There leaning against it was his old buddy, Mike. What did he want? He thought they'd buried the hatchet, or at least had agreed to civility. He surely had heard him spanking Jordyn and really doubted Master Mike would care if he did. So why was he here?

"Hey, there," he said, stashing his tool belt in the case in the bed of the truck.

"Ben," Mike said.

"What's going on? I'm taking this isn't a friendly visit."

He leaned against the bed of the truck and looked at him. Mike was one of the few tall enough to almost look him in the eyes.

Mike looked reluctant, but finally said, "It's Randy."

Great. He didn't need that. "What?" he asked.

"That's the part I don't know," he said. "I just have a feeling and this sounds narcissistic, but I am pretty sure she moved here for me."

"Why do you think that?" Ben had the same opinion but he sure wasn't going to let Mike know that.

"I just, well, I just keep seeing her around. She's bumped into me more times than I've ever bumped into anyone in town. I take my wife out to dinner and there she is. We go to one of Ellie's many events and there she is. Now it could be coincidence, but you and I both know her history."

"Flatter yourself much?" Ben said. "I doubt she's still holding a thing for you after what you did to her."

Mike shrugged. "We both know that often attracts them more than puts them off, but I was young and dumb and couldn't think of anything else to do."

He was right. Something about a good solid paddling made some women crave more and develop feelings. Had Miranda done that? Well, she'd already had feelings for Mike, though for the life of him, he could never figure out why. Sure, they'd dated for a short time, but when Mike broke it off, well, Randy didn't take it well, and apparently had all but stalked Mike for a while. Who would have thought his snooty little sister had such passion in her? Not him. He figured her for the ultimate ice queen, though, really, he tried not to think about it at all.

"So you want me to tell her to stop coincidentally bumping into you?" he asked.

"Yeah, something like that. Just feel her out. I'm happily married now, and really between trying to keep Ellie in line and working, and the new house, I don't have the time or inclination for complications in my life."

Ben understood that. "Your little ball of energy needs keeping in line, does she?" He smiled at Mike and suddenly remembered why they'd been such good friends back in the day.

Mike laughed ruefully. "You would be surprised. I didn't want to come talk to you, Ben, but figured it would be better than talking to her."

"Yeah," Ben agreed. "I'll have a chat with her sometime soon."

He could see the relief on Mike's face. "Thanks, Ben. I really appreciate it."

"You and I both know Randy does her own thing," he warned. "I'm not promising just having a talk with her will do anything, but I'll try."

"That's all you can do," Mike said. "I'll let you get to the BnB. Thanks."

"How did you know where I was going?"

"Bryan took the afternoon off to go out there," Mike said. "He said you were coming to do some estimating."

Of course. "Small town living," he said. "You all have your noses pretty far up each other's butts."

"Just keep Miranda out of mine," he said and turned and walked away.

Great. Why had he moved here again? Oh yeah, fresh start in a new place where the only person he knew was his baby sister. Yeah, that worked out well for him, didn't it?

However as he drove to the edge of town, he thought how much he really liked this town. He loved the energy of it, partly because of Mike's little wife who seemed to run everything. According to Jordyn, Ellie had a big hand in renovating the downtown square, where her shop was going to open. Many towns, their downtown was all but dead, but here, it was thriving with bustling shops and many office buildings. There were about a dozen apartments above the shops, he'd heard. Plus the square held so many events. It would be the heart of the town again, he felt certain. It felt good to be a small part of that revitalization by doing his renovations and repairs. He loved the lake and the fact he could rent a boat and go fishing any time he wanted. Maybe, eventually, he'd buy a house out there. Settle down. Wife and kids? Over the last few days he decided he was finally open to that suggestion again. It had been a struggle, but Jordyn's giggle and braid flipping were a strong part of that decision. She and Laura would have been good friends. He'd felt a sense of peace overcome him while he was considering and felt certain Laura had sent it.

He was in no hurry, but as he pulled up to the sprawling house overlooking the lake that was to be turned into a bed and breakfast he thought he might take Jordyn here on their honeymoon. That gave him six or eight months to lead her in that general direction, and gave him some time to make sure that was what he wanted.

Thinking of carrying Jordyn over the threshold made him smile as he walked up to the door and knocked on it. The wraparound porch seemed sturdy, at a quick glance it only needed a few small repairs and some paint. He needed to get into contractor mode and out of lovesick mode.

"Hi, Ben, come on in." Bryan opened the door. "Jenna is upstairs."

He looked around and smiled. This was going to be a fun job. He'd be renovating his honeymoon suite.

Chapter 6

Jordyn looked up as Jenna walked in the door. "Hi!" She stood up to greet her. "I remember you! Bryan's sister, right? Opening the new BnB out at the lake? Come to check out the competition?"

Jenna, a small blonde, shook her head, and grinned in a way that made Jordyn immediately like her. They'd had dinner together one night at Mike and Ellie's but she hadn't talked to her much. "No, I came to see if the competition needed some help."

Jordyn looked at her, puzzled. "Are you asking if I'm hiring?"

Jenna nodded, her long blonde hair falling in waves. It looked like hers when she took it down after a long day in a braid, but Jordyn suspected that hers was natural and not forced into it. "I got my time estimate back the other day, and it is going to take months to get my BnB up to code and renovated. In the meantime, since I have zero builder person skills, I need to do something. Ben said you were hiring both temporary and part time, and I thought perfect!"

Jordyn wasn't sure how she felt about it. Although, really,

would they be competition? The BnB would be aimed at vacationing people, while she was counting on the town supporting her business for the most part.

"I am hiring," she said. "I need about two more people through the holidays. It would be great if they could bake and work the front with the customers."

"It sounds perfect," Jenna said. "Ben said that the BnB won't be done until probably June, which is just in time for summer reservations, but it is October now! That's a long time to go without a paycheck."

Jordyn, for some reason, liked her. "So have you had baking experience?"

Jenna nodded. "I have worked at hotels since I was fifteen and started cleaning rooms. I've worked my way up and have done everything from front desk, to pool cleaning, to helping with the catered events, including helping with the morning baking before corporate took over and started shipping it all in."

"I imagine that went over well," Jordyn said. "Going from homemade to open the wrapper muffins."

"Sadly, mostly people are used to it. I'm excited to get back into baking again. I'm a quick learner, can follow your recipes, and am pretty handy with a piper. Plus, I have a few people skills. Right now, through the holidays, my schedule will be flexible. I'm very reliable, hotels are open 24/7/365, you know. Then after your grand opening and holiday rush, we can sit down and reassess."

Jordyn laughed. "You have this all figured out, don't you? And Ben sent you!" Weirdly, that gave her a little pang of, well, something. She didn't know what. He was supposed to be working on her renovation, not this new BnB! Was he pawning her off onto someone else? He knew she had to be out of her apartment by end of January. Her landlord had given her a month's grace in lieu of a cake for his parents' fiftieth anniversary. She still had to pay rent for January but she didn't have to move during the Christmas rush or resign her lease for another year. It was a good trade off. She made a mental note to check with Ben about her timeline, but in the meantime, she reached over and grabbed an application form. "Just fill this out with all the details and I'm going to go ahead and say you are hired."

Jenna smiled at her. "I'll look forward to working with you, Jordyn."

For me, Jordyn almost said, but just smiled. "I hope we will be a good team. I've got another person, Moriah who will come in. She's learning to bake, but will mostly work the front area, making coffee and ringing up customers. Then I'm hiring someone else, I hope, tomorrow."

"Is that all?" Jenna asked. "Think that will be enough?"

"I guess we will find out," Jordyn said. "I'm operating on limited hours to start, and then will expand as I figure out the needs and wants of the customers. Right now I'm planning to be open 6 to 2 Monday through Saturday and then 7 to 2 on Sunday. One day to sleep in!" She'd decided to be open seven days a week to start. Last thing she wanted was someone ordering a cake from someone else and not getting into the routine of dropping by for their morning coffee and muffin. Almost all the stores downtown would be hiring extra people for Christmas and she wanted them to know her. She'd worked seven days a week before, and she could do it again.

"I'll bring the paper back tomorrow," Jenna said. "See you then!"

Jordyn watched her walk out the door and shook her head. That one was a little powerhouse. Jenna would make a go of her BnB. Hopefully, she wasn't being stupid hiring her, but since Ben had recommended her, well.

When did his opinion start meaning so much to her, carrying so much weight? Somehow, she just knew he wouldn't steer her wrong or send her someone he thought could be a threat to her business. She trusted him completely, and that was a little scary. What did she really know about him, after all? He was widowed and Miranda's brother and had a penchant for spanking her and making her giggle. Why? Did he maybe treat all the women he worked for that way? He'd remodeled Joni and Beth's bathroom. Had he spanked them? Had he backed Beth up against the wall and kissed her till her ears rang and her knees gave way? Would he be ordering Jenna over his knees soon, then let her cuddle on his lap and take her to dinner?

Jordyn stood up, too many thoughts running through her head. Maybe she didn't want to hire Jenna. Could she stand to hear about her burgeoning relationship with Ben while he worked on the BnB? And what about her apartment? Would he be delegating that out while he romanced the pretty little blonde? What if Jenna came to work all giggly in the morning and not being able to sit down without wincing and, well, Jordyn shook her head.

She needed to stop thinking about Ben and his busy busy social life. Why had she felt special? That wasn't not thinking about him, she scolded herself. She had a business to run.

Looking around her shop, she smiled. It was forced, but it was a smile. This was her life. The only thing she needed to care about at the moment. She'd be doing her soft opening in just a little over a week, then in two weeks would be her grand opening. It had been a long haul, but she was ready! And excited. Ben had nothing to do with either of those things, of course.

Right now, though, she needed to pay some bills. Miranda had sent her the final bill for the shop and she'd be glad to get all that paid for. Once again, she sent a little thanks up to Grandma Rose. How many people could open a shop without a loan? It made her feel good. Picking up the phone she scrolled down and hit the number to the sign shop, hoping they would tell her when it would be shipped. She had the banner ready to hang, but really wanted that permanent sign out front. Beth had come up with a beautiful design for it, but then had refused payment. Jordyn had gotten around that little detail by sending a large bouquet of thank you flowers with an even larger gift card attached. A person deserved to be paid for their work.

Smiling, she finished paying her bills, then got out the estimate that Ben had given her to install a little kitchenette and bathroom upstairs, plus an outside egress, one where she didn't have to come down through the shop to leave or go through it. It was not only required by code – code again – but would be nice if she didn't want people to see her come and go if she took a day off.

Then she frowned. Was he still planning to do her renovation? Or would he be too busy with Jenna and her place? Sighing, she wondered why she cared. What kind of relationship did they have? He thought nothing of just leaving for days without telling her. She just didn't know where she stood with him. Were they even a thing? Or was she just someone he kissed and loved on, spanked and left? He said he wouldn't hurt her again but what did that even mean?

She needed to stop thinking, she told herself firmly. Now. It was getting her nowhere. She closed her bank app and filed all her paperwork, then stood up and moved it all to her new office. This would be where she would do the paperwork and ordering things from now on, so she might as well start getting used to it. Going to the display room, she took the card table down and carried it upstairs. Setting it back up, she smiled. Her first piece of furniture in her new place. She hoped. It would be lovely to be able to have a thirty second commute, especially in the winter. Plus imagine how good her little apartment would smell with all the breads and muffins being baked every morning!

Going back down, she picked up the two folding chairs and carried them up, too. There. The only things in her shop now were shop things. It was starting to feel very real.

She heard a noise downstairs and headed back down, ignoring the flutter in her stomach that told her it might be Ben. No one else had a key and she was certain she locked the door after Jenna left.

What was she going to say to him? What was he going to say to her? Why was she so nervous? Nothing had changed that she knew of. Had it?

Walking in the display room, there he stood, smiling at her through that beard. "Hi, Ben," she said, stopping just to look at him. He was just a fine specimen, wasn't he?

He looked at her and asked, "Is my fly undone or something?"

Jordyn giggled. "If it is, I didn't notice."

"That's disappointing," he said in that teasing tone of voice she enjoyed so much.

"I know. I'm such a disappointment!" See, light-hearted and fun. Nothing more, she guessed, and felt a pang shoot through her.

Ben grinned at her and opened his arms. "Come here, you big disappointment."

She didn't want to. She wanted to resist. Play it cool and hard to get, yet her traitorous feet moved toward him. Okay, what could a hug hurt? Nothing. Everyone needed a hug now and then. That was a simple fact of life. Melting into his arms just felt right.

"You ready for next week?" he asked her.

"What's next week?" Her brain felt a little off with him so close to her and smelling so good.

He chuckled. "Your soft opening and I'm starting on your apartment."

"You are?" She pulled away from him and blinked back tears that had sprung to her eyes. Why? It was ridiculous. She refused to have them.

"Of course I am, why?" He put his finger under her chin and lifted her head so she looked in his eyes. "Jordyn, what's wrong?"

"Nothing," she said, automatically.

He reached back and smacked her bottom. "Don't you lie to me, young lady!"

Taking her arm, he walked her over to one of the new tables and sat her down on the chair. Then pulled one up and sat down across from her. "So, let's try this again. What's wrong?"

A lone tear escaped and traveled down her cheek. He reached up with a finger and wiped it away. "Speak."

Stubbornly, she shook her head. It would sound stupid.

"I can't make it better if you don't talk to me," he said, in a very gentle tone that almost melted her.

Then her back stiffened and she glared at him. "It isn't your job to make me all better," she said.

"That's good to know," he said. "Takes a big load off."

She tried not to smile, but her lips twitched a little. Sighing, she looked at him, and then said, "Well."

"Deep subject," he agreed. "Well, what?"

"Jenna came in."

"Good. She's looking for a part-time job while she's waiting to open her BnB. I mentioned you were hiring a couple of people." He looked at her. "Did she upset you?"

Jordyn shook her head. "No, but, well."

"We already covered that subject," he said. "Am I going to have to paddle it out of you?"

"Are you going to paddle her?" There. She said it.

"Am I going to what?"

Jordyn looked at him. She had no intention of repeating it.

Finally he said, "What did she say to you, Jordyn?"

Shrugging, she looked away from him, her heart pounding and she could feel her palms sweating. What was going to happen here? She couldn't remember ever feeling, well, she didn't know how she was feeling right now. Like her life was about to change in some way? That was dramatic. Was this dramatic?

"Answer me," he said.

She shook her head again.

"Stubborn, are we? You can either tell me now, or I'll break down that wall the fastest way I know how."

Jordyn had no idea what got into her. None. There had to be a disconnect between her brain and her mouth because she simply stuck her tongue out at him. She had never done that. Never! Not even when she was a little kid! It was mortifying! Her hand clamped over her mouth and she could actually feel her eyes widen.

Ben didn't say a word, but reached out, and of course, she was over his knee. "So the quick way to the brain it is," he said, almost conversationally. Jordyn was still so embarrassed over what she did, she didn't even try to fight him, or even to protest.

"You know what's going to happen, right?"

"I'm sorry," she said, forcing words from her mouth. "I'm really sorry."

"If it helps, you are going to be a lot sorrier in about a minute." And with that he brought down his hand on her bottom.

Jordyn flinched but tried to hold still and closed her mouth as tightly as she could so she wouldn't yelp. She deserved this, and apparently wanted it, or otherwise, she wouldn't have been so stupid. She'd take her punishment like a good girl. If she could.

Later, she thought, well, he was efficient. He got straight to the point, didn't discuss anything, just spanked and spanked hard till she was squirming and begging and finally broke down with a sob. He continued for another minute until she wailed, but still refused to beg him to stop. She just wasn't going to do it.

When it was over, she sobbed as if her heart was broken but felt a little better, until she remembered why she was over his knees. And that she was now going to have to tell him. She couldn't handle another one of those right now. He'd never spanked her that hard and fast before. Usually there had been some kind of warm up, at least. Not this time.

He held her close, and cuddled her to him. "You ready to talk now?" he asked after a few minutes.

She shook her head, and whispered, "No, but I will."

"I'm ready," he said and rubbed her back.

Could she do this? Did she have a choice? Not really. "Are you going to spank Jenna too?" she asked him.

He stilled. Was he even breathing? "What?" he asked as if his ears deceived him. Silly male. They hadn't.

"I asked if you, well, am I just one of many?"

"Oh." He relaxed a little bit. "Yes. I kiss and cuddle and make love to and paddle every single woman on every single job. It's kind of my signature. Of course, I have to make sure she's gorgeous first. It's why I rarely work. Hard to find many pretty women who need their stuff fixed."

She balled up her fist, and lightly punched his huge arm. "I'm serious."

"You're ridiculous." He squeezed her again and she tried not to smile or melt.

"Am not."

"Am, too," he said. "Really, Jordyn, is that what you've

been upset about? You think I'm planning to replace you with whoever my next job is? That you're a placeholder?"

She nodded her head vigorously and almost managed to choke back a pitiful sob. It escaped anyway.

"I'm sorry, Jordyn. I never meant to make you feel that way," he said, and began rubbing her back again. She liked it when he did that.

She shrugged. What could she say to that? She couldn't help how she felt.

"Are you planning to mess around with the first customer who comes in and buys cupcakes?"

"What?" This conversation was devolving quickly.

"You heard me."

"No."

"Why not?"

Why not? "Because I'm seeing you."

"Right."

Jordyn shook her head again. That wasn't the same, and he knew it. "I won't be spending days and days and weeks with him in close quarters. And bedrooms," she pointed out.

He laughed. "And you think that's all it takes for me to have a lapse in judgment?"

She shrugged and shook her head again.

He sighed. "Okay, full disclosure."

What did that even mean? "Okay?"

"I was a little wild in college. In fact, Mike and Max and I ran in the same circles. Then I met Laura and everything changed. She was the only one I could see or think about. After she died, I went a little crazy and did go through a few girls. When I moved here though, I hadn't dated or been with anyone for a few years, till you."

"Why me?"

He chuckled, making her smile. She did adore that sound.

It warmed her to her toes, and in a much better way than he warmed her butt. "Fishing for compliments?"

"You like fishing," she said.

"True. Well, I admire your work ethic. I was really impressed with how young you are and what you've accomplished. I like that you have a big group of friends who are like your family. It means you are a good person."

"Or they just tolerate me for my cupcakes," she said.

"That could be," he agreed. "Then you have that cute little nose, and I love the way you flip that braid around. Then when you take your hair down, man. It kills me." He squeezed her again. "You are funny and smart, gorgeous as hell, take your spankings like a good girl, and well, I'm a little smitten."

"Smitten?" she giggled again. "Just a little?"

He grabbed her braid and pulled her head back enough to kiss her, then growled. "Don't question it."

"Yes, Sir," she said, trying to catch her breath.

"Good girl," he said and kissed her again. "Jordyn, we've only known each other a couple of months, and we've both been crazy busy during that time, and really, I don't see that letting up anytime soon, do you?"

She shook her head and felt tears spring to her eyes again. Her emotions today. What was wrong with her? Him. "No, I don't. Between the holidays, and me opening the store and you renovating the new BnB, well. Yeah. Busy."

"And that is our lives, right?"

Jordyn nodded her head. Where was he going with this? Were they breaking up or what?

"So, Miss Jordyn, pretty cupcake lady, do you want to go steady with me?"

Giggles erupted. "Go steady?"

"Yeah, you know. Be exclusive. So you don't have to worry I'm kissing and paddling anyone else. I'll save it all for you, and we can just see where this goes, despite our busy schedules."

"You don't have to paddle me," she protested. "I could be just fine without it."

"Not an option," he said. "Your butt is too perfect not to turn red regularly."

"Regularly?"

"You didn't answer my question," he said.

Jordyn giggled again. "Yes, Ben. I will go steady with you." She stroked his arm. "My mountain man."

"Yours," he agreed, then stood her up and squeezed her butt. "And mine."

"Yours," she agreed.

Epilogue

Beth Sinclair walked out into the warm spring air. It was a lovely May day and she felt like taking a walk. Downtown was only six blocks away and there were no sweets in the house. Today was Friday and there was an entire weekend ahead. Joni had said something about grilling out after she got home from work today, so the least she could do was supply dessert. Luckily, she only worked till noon on Friday, so she had time to walk downtown and grab a dessert from Jordyn's shop.

Walking, she kept looking around, keeping an eye out, while she walked through the quiet neighborhood. She loved living in Clearwater. It wasn't her old life, but it was a safe, happy life. Doing what she wanted when she wanted and what she felt safe doing with no one fussing over her was a wonderful thing. It had been almost three years now, and even she felt safe here now. Cautious but safe.

She got to the downtown square and headed to Jordyn's shop. As she always did, she stopped and looked up at the sign she'd designed for her. It always filled her with nostalgia. Almost like a homesickness.

Being a graphic designer had been her passion and she'd been good at it. Really good. But then, well, it had felt good to do it again. The insurance company paid her very well, and the hours were excellent. Still she missed designing now and then, and the craving was getting stronger to get back to it. She'd done some brochures and flyers and things for her friend Ellie, but those didn't satisfy her much.

Sighing, she walked in the door of the shop, thinking that Ellie wasn't really her friend. She was Joni's friend and they allowed her to hang out sometimes. Did it matter? It was starting to, but right now, she needed cupcakes.

"Beth!" Jordyn called out from behind the display case. "Good to see you!"

"Hello, Jordyn," Beth said. "How's business?"

"Exceeding expectations," she said, and looked around. Then lowered her voice and held out her hand. "Look!"

Beth looked at the sparkling ring Jordyn was flashing. "Are you and Ben engaged?"

Jordyn nodded. "You are the first person I told! Other than my mom and she didn't understand, but, well, it felt right to tell her. I'm telling my sister tomorrow, then announcing to the friends."

Beth smiled but felt a pang. Joni would be one of those friends. She would not be. There would probably be a small party, with Joni, Ellie, Lucy, Izzy, and a few others, but not her. "I won't tell a soul! Congratulations! I'm so happy for you!"

"Thank you." Jordyn all but beamed she seemed so happy. "I can't believe I get to marry my mountain man."

"You were made for each other," Beth said, suddenly tired of the conversation. "Can you give me a dozen Aunt Daisy's oatmeal cookies and a half dozen each of triple chocolate brownie cupcakes, and strawberry cheesecake bites?"

It was less than five minutes before she was out the door into the fresh Clearwater air.

Beth headed home, pondering her life. Was this it? Forever? Just being home and working from home, with an occasional foray into town. No real friends, no real relationships but her sister? Everyone else thought of her as Joni's reclusive sister, if they thought of her at all and Beth suspected that mostly they didn't.

Blending and not being noticed was a good thing when they had moved here. A few years later, though, well, it was starting to get to her. She needed to be with people. Get out of the house. Be whatever it was that passed for normal. Go out to eat. Date.

Beth shook her head, not believing she was actually thinking about dating. But she was and that was normal. Normal. That word kept coming up a lot in her mind lately. Was she ready to be normal instead of, well, what she had been for the last few years? She thought she might be ready. Did she need to wait till she was really ready?

Maybe she'd let her hair go back to her natural color instead of this mousy brown. Grow it down to her waist again, if she could? Find a job in her chosen field of work?

Or maybe not. Nothing had to happen immediately, after all.

Beth sighed and turned down her street. One thing, she did love this old house. It had been their grandmother's and she'd left it to her and her two sisters. Sitting empty for a few years, Ellie had helped them get everything ready before they came down to move in. Sydney had even moved here for a few months before she moved to Chicago to go to vet school. Syd often wondered if their mom, a busy pediatric surgeon, even noticed she'd left home. She needed to call Sydney tonight. It had been a while since they'd talked. Their mom? Well, she'd call when she had the time.

Walking in the front door, she heard music out on the back deck they'd built last year, tearing down the old porch where she and her sisters and their cousins had spent many a long summer afternoon playing. Termites decided it was time for it to go though. There was a time for everything, Beth knew, and felt change was coming. Right now she wanted supper. Joni must have gotten home early and she was glad. Had she eaten today? She didn't remember.

"Joni, I'm home!" she called. "I brought dessert!"

"Beth! Call 911! Now!" she heard Joni scream from the back yard.

Beth suddenly couldn't breathe. Was this it? Should she help Joni or hide? "Now, Beth! Hurry!"

Hitting 911, Beth made a decision and hurried to the patio to save her sister and almost sagged with relief seeing a fire. It was a fire. She saw Joni fanning the flames for some reason and Hank running over from the house next door.

"This is 911, what is the address of your emergency?" a voice said. Beth gave the address and said, "Fire in the back yard. It's gotten out of control."

She hung up and stuck the phone in her pocket, racing back to the kitchen for the fire extinguisher. By the time she got it and got back out, Hank had the garden hose on, and was spraying the fire out. She set the fire extinguisher down and watched him, trying not to tremble. Slowing her breathing, she watched, as if it were a slow-motion movie while her sister and the neighbor ran around with the hose putting the fire out. Why did it look so odd?

Beth noticed in a strange, odd little part of her brain that the firefighters had shown up. Fire people? She wondered, and also wondered what happened to her slow calm breathing. It just seemed to leave, along with coherent thoughts. She kept hearing, over and over, her sister screaming, "Beth! Call 911. Now!" It wouldn't stop. It wouldn't stop. She sank down beside the fire extinguisher and heard a strong buzzing in her ears. What was going on? Smoke inhalation? Why did she feel so strange?

Maybe she'd just take a little nap? There were miniature people all over her yard and there was nothing she could do. Besides, the ringing was getting louder. Her head felt as if it were floating away and she decided to go with it. Why not? Finally her eyes closed and the strange people went away.

"Beth? Beth? Hey, open your eyes. Good girl. Hi, Beth, my name is Nick. Welcome back. How are you doing?"

Beth opened her eyes, wondering where she was and what happened, but saw the bluest eyes she'd ever seen and stopped wondering. Or caring.

The End

Book Four Coming Soon!

Megan McCoy

Megan McCoy lives in the heartland of America, surrounded by corn, soybean fields and hot guys on tractors. At home, she's raising kids, Chinese Cresteds and poodles, training them all with a tender hand and heart, while saving her sternness for the alpha males in her books. Getting up at three in the morning to write leaves her time for a few hobbies - gardening, canning, bike riding, bread baking and taking in strays.

Don't miss these exciting books by Megan McCoy and Blushing Books!

Clearwater Romance series
The Wife He Wanted
The Wife He Adored
The Wife He Needed

Hometown Love series
Don't Mess with Jess
Hannah and Hawk
Totally Tori
Kelly's Haven
Hometown Love Collection

Her Choice series
His Firecracker
The Dilemma

The City Girl
Her Choice, Always
Her Choice Forever

South Dakota Dreams series
Stormy's Trouble
Talia's Time
Wynter's Waif
Wynter's Wife
Sailor's Search
South Dakota Dreams Collection

Along Came Jones Series
Sebastian
Hank
Logan and Ronnie
Logan's Contract
Along Came Jones Collection

Single Titles
Two Weeks of Joy
An Old-Fashioned Relationship
Hard Wired Desires
Quinn's Comeuppance

Anthologies
12 Naughty Days of Christmas 2016
12 Naughty Days of Christmas 2017
12 Naughty Days of Christmas 2020

Audio-Books
An Old-Fashioned Relationship

Connect with Megan McCoy

www.meganmccoy.com

Blushing Books

Blushing Books is the oldest eBook publisher on the web. We've been running websites that publish steamy romance and erotica since 1999, and we have been selling eBooks since 2003. We have free and promotional offerings that change weekly, so please do visit us at http://www.blushingbooks.com/free.

Blushing Books Newsletter

Please join the Blushing Books newsletter
to receive updates & special promotional offers.
You can also join by using your mobile phone:
Just text BLUSHING to 22828.

Every month, one new sign up via text messaging will receive
a $25.00 Amazon gift card, so sign up today!